FICTION   Hruby, Andes.
HRUBY
           The trouble with
           Catherine.

DATE			

The
Trouble with
Catherine

The Trouble With Catherine

A NOVEL BY

Andes Hruby

DUTTON

DUTTON
Published by the Penguin Group
Penguin Putnam Inc., 375 Hudson Street, New York, New York 10014, U.S.A.
Penguin Books Ltd, 80 Strand, London, WC2R 0RL, England
Penguin Books Australia Ltd, Ringwood, Victoria, Australia
Penguin Books Canada Ltd, 10 Alcorn Avenue, Toronto, Ontario, Canada M4V 3B2
Penguin Books (N.Z.) Ltd, 182–190 Wairau Road, Auckland 10, New Zealand

Penguin Books Ltd, Registered Offices: Harmondsworth, Middlesex, England

Published by Dutton, a member of Penguin Putnam Inc.

First Printing, March 2002
10 9 8 7 6 5 4 3 2 1

LIBRARY OF CONGRESS CATALOGING-IN-PUBLICATION DATA

Hruby, Andes.
    The trouble with Catherine / Andes Hruby.
      p.   cm.
    ISBN 0-525-94640-3 (alk. paper)
    1. Fulton Fish Market (New York, N.Y.)—Fiction.   2. Women in business—Fiction.
3. Irish Americans—Fiction.   4. New York (N.Y.)—Fiction.   5. Single women—Fiction.
6. Young women—Fiction.   7. Fish trade—Fiction.   I. Title.

PS3608.R83 T7 2002
813'.6—dc21   2001042191

Printed in the United States of America
Set in Simoncini Garamond
Designed by Leonard Telesca

PUBLISHER'S NOTE
This book is a work of fiction. Names, characters, places, and incidents are either the product
of the author's imagination or are used fictitiously, and any resemblance to actual persons, living
or dead, business establishments, events, or locales is entirely coincidental.

To my grandparents, Paul and Eva Keller,
though neither of you are alive to hold this book in
your hands, I am forever grateful for your faith in me.
Danke für immer Daumen halten.

In memory of The Captain, William J. Lacey
February 3, 1945–April 1, 1999

Contents

1

Summer Showers

At twenty-nine I thought I should marry. If I had known then what I know now, I would have rescued an old dog instead of a young man.

The second Saturday of August, after an endless, irritating summer of soaring heat, I stood in front of forty women who expected me to marry the second Saturday of September. I had doubts about what I was going to do, but I kept thinking that because everyone else wanted the marriage to happen then I should, too. Over the last few years I had adapted my father's fish import business to suit myself, and as I began expanding the responsibility in my career, I also began to notice that all my friends were separating into two camps: married and unmarried. Naively I'd assumed that love and marriage would fall into place just as my career had, but just as I was succeeding in the business world there was a silent movement taking place. The word *independent* fell out of vogue. *Independent,* it seemed, had become the code for "a difficult woman."

All my life I had been slightly ostracized as the dock brat, and in my own way I wanted and hoped that marriage would make me a softer woman. Men don't marry tomboys; they marry women. If I became engaged, it meant that I had outgrown being the tough little brat from her father's fish stall by Pier 17. It meant I had become mature enough to be called someone's wife.

Steve seemed right for me as we read the papers on a Sunday morning months ago. I had the *Daily News,* and he was layered under the *New York Times.* After skimming the headlines I always skip the first few pages and go directly to the gossip column to find out what happened at my clients' restaurants. If it hadn't been for the small typewritten insert I would have missed the ring taped to the top of the column entirely. The ring's unimaginable clarity and platinum band were transparent against the gray-and-black newsprint. He had cleverly written:

Stunning female fishmonger merges with junior partner at Scudder, Scadden, Skipowitz and Dawn. Fans cheered as they walked the plank and leaped into the sunset.

For a moment I pretended not to notice it, and watched Steve's eyes dart methodically back and forth over the top of the business section. I folded my paper in half and held it with my right hand while slipping my engagement finger into the ring. I looked up from the paper and met his eyes with a nonchalant smile, as if nothing unusual had happened. When he slapped the stock report down on the table I could see he was anxious.

"Coffee?" he barked.

"Forever!" I answered, and jumped toward his lap in excitement.

My sudden movement took him by surprise, and he leaned back in his chair. I was moving forward so quickly that my weight toppled him onto the floor. As I extended my arms, to brace myself for the fall, I felt the ring catch on something soft before tearing it. Steve had a deep scratch from the corner of his mouth to his earlobe that pained him for the rest of the day every time he smiled.

The height of the ring and the corners of the setting were something I never grew accustomed to. I often caught it on bras, cuffs of shirts, and the zipper of my pants when tucking anything in. To Steve's credit, he turned the proposal into a great story that always ended with the line: "Imagine? I'm probably the only guy in the world who took a left hook from his fiancée the day he proposed!" I suppose if I had paid attention, I could have foreseen that the scenario would repeat itself.

At my bridal shower I noticed that the married women finished their champagne and let their coffee get cold. I kept my arms elbow-deep in soapy water so no one would see my hands shake. My mother watched every move I made because she knew I had doubts. She'd been suspicious since the moment I showed her the oversize diamond and watched how awkwardly I moved when I wore it.

When someone called attention to my nervous managing of the gifts, she interrupted: "Remember, it can be so overwhelming," and the room let out a soft coo.

I listened to the summary of sounds I made as I had opened my gifts. These are traditionally turned into a short paragraph of "things the bride will say on her honeymoon night." The *oh*s and *ah*s reminded me of how mundane my sex life had become. The closer Steve and I grew to being married, the more I found myself masturbating when he wasn't around. It was an attempt to assert my independence and reassure myself I could live without someone.

When a motherly voice yelled "Cleanup," I watched a ballet of well-trained suburban dancers sweep through the house. Soon the masses of wrapping paper disappeared, the dishes rattled lightly on the wash cycle, and a group of four-cylinder motors started up in unison. As I lay on the living room floor I counted each guest who tapped lightly on the brake to make sure that the extra cookies, quiche, or cake were secure for the drive home. Some women had too much champagne and not enough coffee; their tires squealed briefly when they finally pulled away from the curb. A bouquet of ribbons sat on top of a new box of imported French saucepans. The ribbons had been woven closely together. I tugged at each loose string, like a kitten.

My dear friend, Monica, took them from my hands and said: "Don't tear those apart. We need them for the rehearsal dinner."

The nugatory details of a proper marriage kept me drowning in wedding etiquette books written by women I would have ignored at dinner parties. I wanted to pull Monica aside and ask if I had done all right. I had been at her wedding shower and witnessed her amazing ability to deal with a gaggle of women like a bird trainer. For many of my friends it seemed natural, but for me it was like being surrounded by pigeons, all pecking at me.

The entire summer had swept by in a flurry of weddings. Everyone I knew was suddenly more concerned with china patterns than with careers, and they were all in therapy to help make the transition. The red flag was waved a few laps before thirty, and we ran for the matrimony finish before anyone could call us *spinsters.* No one used that word, but it lurked in my mind as the heat rose higher in August and my relationship cooled. I imagined myself with silver braided hair, wearing a pair of fish-gut-stained overalls, an embroidered sweater, and some old rubber boots, still wondering if the company made more money selling high-end tuna or cheap fillets.

If marriage wasn't the immediate option, most of my "live-together" friends suddenly bought garden apartments in Brooklyn, Westchester suburbs, or New Jersey town houses. Advice books on finding the right man were strewn across every apartment that had more than one woman living in it, and I was reminded of how badly I had conducted myself in many relationships. The most honest advice I received was from a business acquaintance, the only thirty-six-year-old woman I knew who had opted not to marry. At the time I was too young to appreciate what she was saying, but I never forgot it as the years went by.

We were having dinner in a chic Manhattan restaurant when she said: "I made a mistake."

"How do you know?"

"Because I'm about to be a lot older than Jesus and no one wants to take me to the altar."

"I'm more concerned with import taxes," I said.

"Become a wife and stop trying to run your father's business. You'll wind up spending more time on plastic surgery than shoe shopping."

Marriage was not on my agenda. I was having too much fun being single.

"You're twenty-five, right?" asked Jean.

"Right."

"Take my advice: Start now. You must practice looking for a partner every time you go on a date. Date several men intensely for one year, and if none of them asks you to marry him, move on to the next."

"Are you serious?"

"Deadly! Didn't your mother tell you any of this?"

"No, she was raised in a Catholic school, and nuns are much more concerned with keeping young women away from men than teaching them how to catch them."

"Are you Catholic?"

"Yes."

"Well, that's it."

"What?" I asked.

"If you were raised in a Protestant home you would know that when women drink a few martinis their favorite subjects are all the men they didn't sleep with—and the men someone else married."

"So?"

"People who believe in *God* look for soul mates. The rest of us look for a strong gene pool and someone who has initials we can remember after cocktails."

"Come on."

"Fine, don't believe me. I knew the rules at your age, but I rebelled against them. Now I have suffered."

"What rules?" I asked.

"Twenty-seven is the last stop on the single train. You might get a little bit of leeway until you turn twenty-eight, but don't stay single too long after that, because it's an express ride to thirty. Then, the only route left is the one bound for the classifieds."

"What do you do at twenty-nine if you don't have a ring?" I asked.

"Then you can option the Lemon Law. You take three months to keep a relationship or turn it in. Don't date anyone who isn't ready to start planning a wedding after three months."

"Where are you in all of this?"

"I've got to put up with being single for two more years."

"But then you'll be thirty-eight."

"I'll be in the market for the best of the worst."

"Which is?"

"Divorcés who already went to therapy."

I should have waited for the divorcés to roll around, but instead I became the one-date wonder. The list of traits and idiosyncrasies that I wanted in a partner was so long it became a joke among my friends. I was searching for the impossible because I didn't really want a husband. The list was the only way I could pretend I felt the same panic as everyone else and was out there looking for someone instead of just screwing the ones I liked.

"Was his shirt tucked in?"

"Yes."

"Was he wearing a belt?"

"No," I said.

"Did he ask you out again?"

"Yes."

"Are you going?"

"No belt, no second date."

"Didn't he run a marathon?"

"Yes."

"So? Why no second date?"

"No belt, no second date," I said firmly.

"You are high maintenance."

"I don't plan to change."

When I met Steve he fulfilled more requirements on my list than anyone else had thus far. He had lived in a foreign country, spoke a second language, polished his shoes, manicured his nails, sent his laundry out, trimmed his pubic hair, brushed his teeth (and aspired to floss), ate meat, drank alcohol, liked dessert, ran a marathon, wasn't fussy about body fluids, had no male pattern baldness in his family, was over six feet tall, never showered after sex alone, graduated from a good law school, liked the seasons, enjoyed science fiction and detective movies, hoped to someday practice yoga, wanted a dog, didn't like cats, and thought that one child was enough. I couldn't dismiss him on any real grounds. Previously I'd preferred men who tied me to chairs and painted my body, but my arousal from being stroked by an artist's wet paintbrush ended when I couldn't wash off a crimson red landscape from my neck to my toes. I had to tell everyone I had tried a home spa soak in beet juice that was supposed to shrink cellulite.

My friends were delighted to see me dating someone who wore pants without paint on them to the dinner table. They embraced Steve immediately and chose to overlook his career choice as a corporate lawyer. Our first few dates gave me no inclination to what his social world comprised. We had been set up by a man I knew from the New York Runner's Club. Steve and I had similar marathon paces, and he was eager to find someone who he could train with in the early mornings. I had always lost time during the marathon on the last few miles from the north end of Central Park until the finish because of the slight uphill grade. Although every year I knew it was essential for me to train in the park, it was so far from where I lived, and training alone was an invitation for rape. Neither Steve nor I had ever tried running with a partner, and the idea appealed to us both—especially after our first flirtatious conversation. Neither of us seemed to make an effort to comb our hair or look especially appealing at five-thirty in the morning, but we were stripped of anything that could have warned us that we came from different worlds. We had running watches, technically efficient sneakers, a few nice sweatshirts, and worn baseball hats. The first time he asked me out for supper we were to meet at an uptown social club where he was a member. Upon arrival I was informed I could not be served in the restaurant because I was wearing slacks; women were required to wear skirts in the main dinning hall.

I should have known better then, but as our wedding date grew closer the problems between us were growing into chronic character differences instead of minor conflicts. A man who has never known blue-collar labor is not a man who should marry a woman who has spent her summers gutting fish or hauling crates onto trucks. He repeated the best lines from the *New York Times* at cocktail parties, and I swore that the real stories were to be heard on the docks. Although Steve claimed he cherished my quirks, as time passed he no longer defended me. As I struggled through long tedious barbecues on the tip of Long Island that hot summer, I realized that he had changed his position, and I could see that he hoped I would buy the pastel-colored slippers all the other women wore instead of always opting for comfort in my shoddy deck shoes.

With each wedding I had begun to see flaws in our social structure. Brides got drunk and cried about lovers they didn't marry. The single guys swarmed the bar and avoided dancing with anyone in a taffeta bridesmaid dress. Every woman wanted to catch the bouquet, but no man was eager to raise a hand for the garter. A disturbing rumor was running amuck that the stress of getting married usually led to a night of sexless insomnia or extreme drunkenness. Children seemed to be the only ones who really had a good time at weddings; caterers cleared plates filled with vegetables while the kids ate wedding cake drowned in maraschino cherries they stole from the bar.

I had already been involved in two outdoor weddings. The first one was during July at the start of the summer heat wave. By ten a.m. I had soaked through a cobalt-blue bridesmaid's dress. Large crescent moons of sweat grew under my arms and breasts. The photographer had all of us in the bride's party turn profile and keep our arms at our sides so the stains wouldn't show. During that reception three people fainted. The champagne glasses were so moist that one slipped out of the best man's hands during the toast and smashed on the floor. The band went stale because no one danced. Men and women hung out in the bathrooms inside the hotel to soak up the air-conditioning. No one paid attention to the sequence of scheduled events. Half the guests were inside at the bar when the bride and groom wanted to cut the cake.

The bride, Monica, threw her hands up and stopped trying to make it all work. It was her day, and she wasn't having fun. She called her bridesmaids together for a quick meeting in the bathroom near the bar. We each stripped down to our slips and push-up bras, chugged cold beers, ran through the lobby, the tent, and then headed off to the estate's pool.

We ran through the center of the buffet and in between its decorated tables, giggling, squealing, and cackling like little witches. There must have been a quiet moment of shock before anyone moved. The cacophony of silverware meeting plates died altogether.

The photographer raised his camera and photographed us running down the hill toward the pool. In the photo, six of us trail behind Monica in her veil. We are far enough away to look like deer in a field. In the dusky light our gauze slips and bare legs appear to be stark white tails dancing across the lawn.

The groom's party soon followed and encouraged the entire wedding entourage down the hill to the pool. Ceremoniously, all the newlyweds' parents held hands and marched down the steps into knee-deep water. For the first time in twenty-three years Monica saw her divorced parents hold hands. The wedding cake was served by the pool on plastic plates, and we played volleyball with our flower arrangements until it was time for the bride and groom to head off in the limousine. Those of us already engaged were accustomed to giving our bouquets away to waitrons, while the bride tossed her bouquet to random cousins and women she barely knew, who were filled with hope.

There was no break in the temperature for Beverley's wedding a month later. The heat soaked further into the crevices of concrete and tar, by the last week in August agitating the city's surfaces like a latent volcano. Summers that hot bred discontent.

Beverley had given up a good job in a Vermont mail-order company to stay in New York with Darnel. Marrying Darnel meant she was marrying New York City. Darnel promised her a life with a garden, and within a few months he found a beautiful old brownstone in Brooklyn. The garden plot had knee-deep weeds and a kiddie pool abandoned by the previous tenant. Beverley saw a fertile field enclosed in concrete waiting for that touch of love once she wheeled away the plastic pool in a shopping cart. Love has amazing power when it's on your side.

All Beverley wanted for her nuptials was to be surrounded by nature, even if it was only through a glass-bottom vase and color scheme. The bridesmaids wore green dresses the shade of fresh onion grass, and Beverley wore an iris-tinted gown with a yellow veil. As we collected in the small hall inside a Brooklyn church every breeze blew pollen around the room and caused an opera of sneezes. Only Beverley's hearty Vermont lungs were accustomed to such high pollen counts. Everyone who lived south of Westchester County spent the day sniveling into their cloth dinner napkins and sneezing into the bread baskets.

The bartender acquired a bottle of antihistamines, and if you tipped him well, he slid one to you with your beverage. Taking over-the-counter drugs and drinking champagne created a party of wired drunks. When the caterers begged us to leave, we moved from the wedding hall into the honeymoon suite. We deprived the bride and groom of consummating their wedding by playing drinking games like I Never and Six Degrees of Kevin Bacon until the sky was light again.

Before Steve, I did not need to love someone to have sex with him, nor did I care if a man I slept with called me back. I left more men in bed with the sheets still warm than those I cared to spend the whole night with. I would have dated nice boys if they knew how to have naughty sex.

For my friends, my escapades were sources of vicarious infidelity; they called me Crazy Catherine. They listened to my stories of wild times, sexual antics, hard liquor abuse, and even drug experiments, without ever being unfaithful to their own relationships. When my friends believed they had misbehaved they called on me first; it was rare they could outdo me in confession. When I stayed with Steve for more than six months, everyone seemed so happy to see that I'd settled down that I continued to want their approval. I was tired of defending my choices. My dates and lovers had always been the amusement of others at dinner parties. Steve was single and heterosexual. He had no children and no diseases. He had health benefits and a plan for retirement. I was becoming part of a group of friends that was expanding as "couples." Now, like the rest of my friends, I, too, worried about how to arrange the closets if we moved in together. I told secrets about Steve's personal habits, and my friends also told me things that drove them crazy about their new husbands. I was becoming one of the "girls" for the first time in my life.

Emily was the next person to marry that summer in the slow suffocating sauna. She went from being a solid-minded, savvy, and frugal woman to a lavish, extravagant Southern belle. Planning a wedding is like getting really drunk; all the things you would never do or say suddenly come very easily. A wedding is the hidden key to learning about your friends. It is either the reflection of who you thought they were or the idealized dream of what they want to be. In either case, over the past few months I had grown unable to recognize Emily at all.

I concentrated on making conversation that did not involve my wedding arrangements. The long list of petty bits and pieces, table arrangements, and thank-you-note stationery that brides were supposed to enjoy deciding upon was unbearable. It was the last thing I wanted to discuss during my time off from work. I had become so annoyed and vexed by Emily's constant banter about her nuptials that I would sigh and roll my eyes when we spoke on the telephone. Had I been more willing to see the faults in my own situation I might have foreseen I was jealous that she enjoyed the process of planning her wedding, whereas to me it had become just a burden.

There was a strange mix of people at her wedding. Half of them were Emily's age, a frustrated group of late-twenty-some-things who had not quite made their mark, and the other half remembered The Beatles and Kent State. Emily's fiancé was a sweet, bright man who had been one of her professors. His friends had impressive educations and low-paying teaching jobs. They were the type of people who trained themselves to be so politically correct that they called the bartender an "independent contractor."

The start of the wedding was delayed. Most of us had become so accustomed to our repetitive pew positions that it took some time until we noticed the harpist had played the wedding march six times, and the "independent contractor" started serving drinks in the cocktail lounge adjoining the reception tent. In my aggressively despondent state of mind regarding matrimony, I was the first to conclude we would never see her in the dress and shoes that matched the catering, floral arrangements, chair ribbons, and Asian-infused kosher menus.

After an hour Beverley looked over at me and said: "Should we go see what happened?"

My tolerance was low. I had been angry with Emily since she decided to stick her two sisters in the bridesmaids' gowns and didn't ask us to stand by her. I felt if she needed someone now, she had her sisters. Beverley was more generous.

At the back of the small inn, up a narrow dark hallway, we found the bridal suite. We knocked on the door, twice.

One of her sisters answered, half-dressed. "What?"

"We wanted to make sure everything was all right," I said.

"Of course it's all right," she snapped back.

"You're an hour past schedule," said Beverley.

Emily's older sister closed the door and said: "Have another drink, we'll be there."

We were astonished. Back in our seats without collaborating a story, we said in unison, "Have another drink, she'll be here."

An additional fifteen minutes developed into half an hour when one of her sisters finally spoke to an usher. Suddenly, all at once we rose and watched Emily enter under a parasol. There was a small gasp from Beverley, and I grabbed her hand; Emily stood erect with her shoulders thrown back. On top of her simple rose tinted veil was a gaudy rhinestone tiara. She stood next to her aggravated father, as if they were about to go trick-or-treating.

When her gray-haired father delivered her to her gray-haired groom, I held Steve close and loved him for being different from my family.

The first time our parents met we did everything to prevent disaster. We picked a neutral restaurant that was famous for their steaks and stayed far away from country clubs and fresh catch locations. I knew my father would find fault with the parade of material goods Steve's father, Steve Sr., lavishly enjoyed. My mother would find Gail, Steve's mother, irritating every time she decided she absolutely *must* take her to her favorite salon for a treat. I had undergone several salon treats at Gail's special spa that left my skin raw or windburned. What Steve (Jr.) and I could not foresee was that random events and fate would create a detailed police sketch somewhat haunting and uncomfortable for everyone involved.

My parents were already downtown at the office with me after an exhausting round of Saturday morning deliveries I made when a freighter I expected on Thursday didn't clear customs until after midnight on Friday. Steve Jr. had gone up to his parents with the weekend traffic and spent Saturday golfing with Steve Sr. The dichotomy of a day spent delivering fish or swinging golf clubs already set a bad tone, and I called Steve Jr. in a panic at three o'clock and begged him not to come. He ignored me. Steve Sr. was too eager to drive his newest SL class Mercedes Roadster convertible down the turnpike. If Gail hadn't put her leather handbag with signature chain-link shoulder strap behind her before Steve Sr. lowered the convertible top, maybe the fabric roof wouldn't have ripped open when Gail pulled her purse free from the folds to retrieve a token.

By the time Steve Sr. arrived he had lost his after golf glow, and my father had strong shadowy chin stubble since he had been fighting meter maids since six in the morning. Steve Sr. refused to leave his new but slightly wounded convertible in the garage I use to guard my own vintage Mustang. Instead Steve Sr. invited my father to drive across the Brooklyn Bridge to Peter Luger Steak House in his favorite little *toy.* I watched my father cringe at the affectionate term for the car and then gently strap himself into the passenger seat. They were far ahead of us by the time Gail began complaining that there were no rear seat belts in the 1964 Mustang. Steve fought me, as always, on who should drive. No other person has driven the car except my parking attendants and the old man who sold it to me. Thwarted, he rode in the passenger seat for the second time that day and pouted. We missed the accident that Steve Sr. caused, but for the rest of my engagement I would be able to picture every moment of it.

Steve Sr. talked to people with a familiarity that included shoulder punching and backslapping. Although my father was a congenial man, this false sense of intimacy reminded him of insurance agents. It appears that Steve Sr. was reenacting a joke about a monkey, his testicles, and a shotgun when he drifted from the far left passing lane into the middle. There he wedged his right headlight into the rear bumper of a 1976 Ford Pinto with seven turbaned men hidden inside.

After having inspected his car Steve Sr. shrieked: "You bastards can't drive with sheets sliding over your eyes!"

My father, immigrant blood close to a boil, yelled: "Not everyone can watch where *you* drive since you don't pay attention."

My father always made it clear when reenacting the story that he found Steve Sr. to be the kind of man who thought so fondly of himself that he believed people should watch him at all times.

No one from the Pinto could produce a New York State driver's license or insurance card. It was obvious by the thick water in their eyes that Steve Sr.'s threats and rage made them think of a place they did not want to return to. When Steve Sr. flipped open his mobile telephone, my father intervened.

"What in God's name are you doing?" he asked.

"Calling the police."

"What for?"

"I need a police report for my insurance."

"No cop is going to come halfway out on the Brooklyn Bridge to look at a broken headlight unless someone's head is attached to it."

"That is a selective choice halogen bulb manufactured solely for the luxury class models of Mercedes."

"So that's it? You want a new headlight for your little toy?"

"Those falafel heads are going to buy me a new set of two-thousand-dollar headlights or go to jail where they belong!"

"I think they belong in Palestine, but they weren't happy there. Did you forget? This is the land where we take the hungry, the battered, and even those who can't afford lightbulbs that blind you from every angle of the road."

"How can you defend those parasites? They're probably rap-ing our system! The system I built for my retirement with my taxes. I could probably buy a new set of titanium golf clubs with the money they hustle off food stamps!"

My father saw seven men with dirty nails and scars lashed across their hands from hot machinery. Their clothing was spot-ted by thick grease; the knees of their work pants were thread-bare. My father loathed beggars but had a large heart for the workingman. It was just about this time I could see Steve Sr.'s car on the bridge. The long line of merging traffic honked, and driv-ers waved their arms in irritation, and it was then I realized our fathers were holding everyone up.

Since I was driving only six miles per hour I clearly saw my fa-ther reach into his pocket and count out twenty one-hundred-dollar bills and hand them to Steve Sr. My father was the type of man who never joined a club, a hotel chain, or owned a credit card because he didn't like limitations set upon him. He kept large stacks of bills at his disposal to guarantee he could make his own rules. I'm sure he planned on paying for dinner, and I was also sure he had another stack of bills nestled in his shoes if Steve Sr. decided to order expensive champagne or aged wine. Gail dis-tracted me from Steve Sr.'s reaction to the money with her alarmed squeaking noises when she, too, realized her husband had been in an accident. By the time we were parallel with their car, my father had returned to the passenger seat and waved for us to continue on.

While Steve Sr. refused to allow the valet to park the car, we questioned my father.

He quietly remarked: "I lost a little bet about how much a set of titanium golf clubs cost."

A coldness permeated the conversation for the rest of the

evening, but Gail never noticed because she had a list of things my mother absolutely *must* do.

On the way home from Emily's wedding I felt guilty for being angry at her. Her desperate attempt to make the wedding such an important turning point in her life saddened me more than I expected. Those hour-long telephone calls about the dress-shoes-caterer were just her way of asking "What am I doing?" I was ashamed that I mocked her over the past few months as I realized that marriage helps to heal wounds from our pasts.

At each of those weddings the obstacles of the events never affected the love between the bride and the groom. The more I learned about Steve's character by organizing our nuptials, the more I doubted he was right for me. I had to find some way of understanding if my own frantic reluctance was a burst of latent feminism, or part of a real problem with Steve, *before* the final fitting of my dress.

2

Forever Hold Your Peace

What first attracted me to Steve were the bright moons at the base of his manicured nails. He was the exact opposite of my unkempt father. Even when we ran in those early mornings he smelled like soap and laundry detergent. To be close to Steve was to feel clean—yet under his tailored exterior he was often raw and sexy. He was a little rough behind closed doors, cursing or dominating me when we had sex. When we went to cocktail parties I would entertain myself with the secret of his deviant side. This seemed to draw him down to my level of street survival, and it wasn't until much later that I considered he might be a misogynist. I was raised in a rough Brooklyn neighborhood that had fights, cliques, and solidarity in a neighborhood accent. We cursed and fooled around and controlled each other by name-calling and teasing. The girls I knew had anal sex on a regular basis and avoided intercourse so they remained virgins for their wedding nights, but the women in Steve's circle discussed sex like trade merchants. Whenever they were wearing expensive new gifts they would tease each other and ask, "Did you let him do it there?" They acquired watches, pearls, shoes, vacations, earrings, and some were even promised matrimony.

I walked into the small den that overlooked a corner of the East River. Steve was absorbed by his paper and a slowly sinking old couch I had at one time recovered, but for lack of interest never reupholstered. From a distance the couch appeared firm and well put together, but when you tried to make yourself comfortable the pillows dropped through to the floor.

"When is that formal party we have to attend at your firm?" I asked.

"Which one?"

I peeked over the top of the paper and then pulled it down so I could see his face. "The one at Christmas." I held the top of the paper between two sets of fingers, ready to tear it in half.

"Be nice," he said.

"It's yesterday's paper."

"I haven't had a chance to read it."

"When is the party?"

"The tar is melting on the roof and you're worried about what parties we're going to attend in December?"

"Don't be condescending. I have a lot of extra orders to fill at that time of year. I need to plan ahead and make sure things run smoothly."

"Let your father do it?"

"It's my job."

"Should I get up from this couch, put down my paper, interrupt what I'm doing, and call my secretary on a Sunday afternoon because you need an answer *now?*"

He tried to stand gracefully without crumpling the paper or falling back into the couch, but was not successful. The paper creased between two pillows, and when he finally pulled the newsprint from the couch it looked like a strange origami bird, which he threw at me forcefully.

"What the hell is going on with you?" I asked.

He stood over me: "I'm tired of commands disguised as questions."

"What?"

"Everything about the wedding is done before I even give you my final opinion."

"Steve, that's unbearable! You made the final decision about where we had the wedding. You made the final decision about who we invited. You even booked our honeymoon without consulting me!"

"I consulted you!"

"Searching the Internet for the locations your firm has timeshare condominiums is not what I call making a mutual decision."

Steve left the room for a moment, and I could hear him going through drawers and papers on my desk. I heard him go to the refrigerator and get a beer. The last piece of hot sun descended behind a pier. Steve threw a few brochures in my lap and a sketch of the proposed wedding cake. His beer sprayed slightly on the newspaper when he twisted open the bottle.

"Who made all those decisions?" he asked.

I flipped through a list of bands, menus, cake, and champagne choices. "I didn't know you resented my choices," I said.

He brought the cold bottle of beer to his forehead. "Sometimes you talk to me like I just jumped off the turnip truck." I started to stand up but he put out a hand to stop me. "I've been a man for thirty-two years, and I was very good at it until we got together."

"You! But I—"

"You want to prove you can handle the business? Fine. Let it go there. Can't you just back off after five o'clock and let me wear the penis?"

"I didn't know . . ." But of course I did. This argument wasn't about who chose the cake or the honeymoon destination. It was about my need to enforce my independence, my need to prove I didn't need help.

"You do *know*. You get off on putting me down. I bust my ass every day in one of the biggest law firms that exist, and there is a good shot I could make partner this year. Somewhere between you bossing me around and always having to be in control I have lost my ability to feel sexually attracted to you entirely."

I felt tears running down my checks. There was no wheezing or anticipated crying; it was just a rush of water pouring from my eyes. It was one of those moments where the truth hurts so badly your eyes water but you are completely convinced you feel nothing.

"Can you answer one question?" he demanded.

"Maybe."

"Did you buy a dress for our wedding?"

I could feel my arms begin to tremble.

"Did you buy a dress for our wedding? Did you?"

I thought about the long tulle train, the tight stiff bodice, the heavy polyester that was aged to look like turn-of-the-century satin. I had two fittings down and one to go. That dress was mine no matter what happened. Tears ran off my chin at the collarbone.

"It has a six-foot train," I said in between heaves. "I can't return it!"

He put his arms under my knees and armpits and carried me into the bedroom. We sat on the edge of the bed until I stopped crying.

"I'm sorry, honey. I didn't mean to scare you by yelling. I just wanted to know that you were really wearing a dress."

I buried myself into his neck.

"You're just so hard, Catherine. Sometimes I wonder what gets through to you," he said.

"You do," I said softly, knowing it was a lie I was telling both of us because I did not have the strength to end our engagement right then.

"I'd like to think so, Catherine, but I'm not so sure," he said.

His satisfied tone of voice made me feel pitied, not understood. He felt sorry for the little girl who had been scrambling around on the docks and skipping school. He thought he could save me, but I wasn't sure I wanted to be rescued.

He brought his lips to mine. I could feel him wanting me, pulling me tighter and starting to lust after me with his confidence. I surrendered, but as I slipped my tongue across his teeth I could feel my throat tighten. Our lovemaking became a struggle, each of us wrestled violently to be on top. It was rough not passionate. Steve used his size and strength against me; he stopped at nothing to show me his dominance and pinned my arms over my head. He held me down with no regard for my discomfort and drove himself so hard inside me I gasped from the pain. He began cursing at me and then demanding to know if I was going to be his good little girl or just his fuck toy. As he spoke his eyes were closed, and I understood that he didn't know for himself which he believed I was. He continued with a long stream of threats and obscenities until he ejaculated with such force his body shivered. As he lay on me his words ran through my mind. Even with all my rough boyfriends and promiscuous behavior, I had never allowed anyone to demoralize me. Steve curled up next to me. He pulled my body into the sweat on his chest and ran his hands through my hair.

"That was perfect," he said.

We spent the early evening napping and turning up the air conditioner. Although I was the one who had wanted relaxed time together, my mind was racing toward Monday. I could see that the whole situation with Steve had put me on edge, and I needed to call Susan. She was still on San Francisco time but would be headed back East by the end of this week to Pennsylvania for her own wedding preparations; I knew it would be easier to reach her in the morning.

Steve and I decided to go running before dinner. A couple who exercised together supposedly stayed together. I wasn't at the point yet where I could spend four hours on the golf course with Steve. Running was our couple sport. I became a runner to calm myself after the heated hours with my father in our office. Running helped me slip away into places where my mind was quiet and free. When I began to run marathons I realized that people all politely smiled at each other and rarely spoke; it was the largest collection of loners you could ever find at one event. After numerous prep-talks and injury prevention lectures I was a stickler about pacing and form. Steve was still part of the no-pain-no-gain clique.

"What are you thinking about?" asked Steve.

"Nothing," I said, trying to negotiate the upturned cobble surfaces of the fish market.

"There is no such thing as *nothing*."

"I think we're going too fast."

"You can run at my pace."

"This is not healthy."

"My joints thank you, but my fat does not," he said.

"Do you want the long list of reasons why you should not continually work at eighty-five percent of your maximum heart rate?"

"Do you import fish or did you receive a degree in exercise physiology?"

I could feel tightness in my hip and began to slow down.

"Don't do that!" snapped Steve.

I ran even slower. He ran ahead of me and then jogged back to where I was comfortably running along the water.

"Satisfied?" he asked.

"I'll find my way home," I said.

"Don't do this."

I stopped altogether.

"You are stubborn to a fault," he said.

"I exercise for life, not for you."

"Why are you doing this?"

I ran in another direction. When I thought I was going too fast and Steve should be right behind me, I stopped. He had chosen the other direction. It was dark and I was alone. At night, if I am in my running clothes, I feel the city against my skin. I consider myself to be tough, but there is nothing like a shadow along a building to make me admit my frailty in spandex pants after dark. These are the few times I remember I am not my father's son.

On the corner of Fulton Street the tourists' shops had cleared the last of their summer sale items off the cobblestone walk and locked their doors. I walked down to Pier 17, hoping that later, I wouldn't have to break into my own apartment building. Steve carried the keys when we ran because he liked to hear them jingle to the cadence of his step. Being annoyed with me he would run farther to "teach me a lesson." I kept walking since I knew I'd only have to wait for him to come home. We lived on the second floor of a renovated brownstone above the fish shop. The third floor had been used for storage and my first apartment, but my mother was slowly remodeling it. I believe she saw the promise of a child's room in the old slanted attic roof. Steve was in the process of deciding if he wanted to rent or sell the apartment he owned on the Upper East Side; *he* planned to make the third floor his home office.

The salty dirty air stirred memories as I wandered on the pier. I had spent so much time on the docks as a little girl I could hear the echo of my childhood between the rotting pylons. There was the spot I kissed some of the Italian dock boys and wondered if my father really did talk to the barnacles to find out what I was up to.

For the majority of my childhood, twin replicas of Robert L. Fulton's ships were docked at Pier 17. One had been transformed into a hospital ship and the other was owned by a cantankerous young drunk everyone called The Captain. The Captain had inherited the steamship replica from his father as well as any rights for food concession sales on the pier. The problem with the seaport was that in the transitions from generation to generation, the deals had been done by handshake. It was impossible for anyone to prove who really owned things. The City of New York and The Captain had been in a legal battle for more than ten years to decide who would turn the seaport into a tourist attraction.

My father and The Captain liked each other. I followed them on long walks around the sinking ship, listening to the endless bilge pump. During the summers, when I had to work the docks,

The Captain allowed me to roller-skate and practice tap dancing (a short-lived passion) on the ballroom floor. A cool breeze always blew from the East River through the ballroom.

I knew every room, stairway, air vent, and porthole on that ship. It helped me understand the way men gave names to automobiles, lawn mowers, and television sets. The affection I had for the large model steam engine made me slap the side of her hull and say things like, "How ya doing, old girl?"

There was nothing better to me than a night alone on that ship. Even the neighborhood Mafia kids were afraid to stay on the boat once the sun went down, but I thrived listening to the lapping of the waves against the starboard steel.

There was a sense of wonder and loss on the *Fulton*. Old unused mirrors held the memory of women crammed in the bathrooms applying lipstick. If I stayed on the ship long enough after the hustle of the day, and the squawking fishmongers had gone away, I thought I could hear the old crooning songs of the forties through the grooves of the dance floor. The rocking of the large ship would lull me into a dream.

The floor of the ballroom was always dirty and cold. I lay down in the center, waiting for the moment the seaport was quiet and I could drift into fantasy. I had only a short time to warm the boards under my back and enjoy the silence before my father would finish his banking and we'd head back to Brooklyn.

One day I fell asleep. I never heard my father call out for me, or felt the sun drop, nor did I notice the wind had picked up dangerously on the water. I had escaped deep into my imagination and was dancing across the ballroom floor in a silk dress with some sailor I'd never see again.

It was probably just past dinner when one of the large doors from the kitchen to the ballroom swung open. There were no lights on, but I knew each squeak of the abandoned hinges. The dry sound of rotting rubber dragged across the bottom of the moldy carpet as it swung back and forth. Someone else's breath was in the room. The familiar sundown stagger of The Captain glided around the outside of the dance floor. He began to move slowly to the left and then to the right. I realized by the way he held his arms that he imagined a body next to him. He took two steps back and two steps forward, adding a small spin on his right and left heel. He began to sing, nothing I knew or recognized, but it was a song about ruin.

The Captain bumped into chairs and tables covered in dust cloths, but never came toward the center of the dance floor. He circled around the edges like a shark. Part of me wondered if he knew I was there and chose to ignore me or if he was just too drunk to notice. His steps grew slower, and he lit a cigarette.

"Couldn't you county screwballs wait?"

I sat up.

He pulled up a fallen oak chair and relit the cigarette. He smoked long thin Sherman cigars, and his hand shook if he hadn't had enough to drink. I smoked my first cigarettes here with a sailor bound for Singapore, and I made ten bucks from one of the boat guards by ripping a crab in half in front of some unsuspecting tourists. If I had a hundred memories on the boat, The Captain must have a thousand more.

"Couldn't you fucking wait to drag it out of here?"

"It's Catherine."

"Peanut?" he said into the dark.

"I fell asleep."

"What the hell are you doing here?"

"I like to lie down on the ballroom floor sometimes after a hot day working on the docks," I said.

"How the hell did you get in here?"

Throughout the past year, I had gone through all the drawers in the navigation room and put together my own set of keys.

"The window by the door to the kitchen has a piece of broken glass I can slip in and out of place. Then I reach my hand in and open the door. When I'm done I put the glass back."

"Catherine, you can gut a fish quicker than any woman I know, but you're a lousy liar." He sat back on the chair and withdrew a small flask from his pocket.

"I stole a set of old keys from the navigation room."

"Want a drink?" he asked.

"I haven't eaten," I said.

"What the hell does that have to do with it?" He laughed until he choked on his own cigarette smoke. The Captain coughed brutally into his palm and bent over between his knees.

I stood up, unsure if I should help him or run. Men like him are trained to feel your fear. He was immediately quiet and drank slowly from the flask before holding it out to me.

"Have you seen my father?" I asked.

He shook the flask lightly at me and smiled. "Drambuie. It's sweet. You'll like it."

The flask was warm from his breast pocket, and I smelled the thick substantial alcohol. I wasn't much of a drinker at thirteen, but I liked sweet things. The small sip I took wasn't enough to get me tipsy, but it satisfied my curiosity. I considered my only escape from pointless conversation would be to make sure The Captain drank every last bit of that alcohol.

He eyed me carefully, examining the fish guts on my sweatshirt and tar on my sneakers.

"For a woman, you're not much of a lady," he said.

"For a Captain, you don't sail much."

"Your father is down at the corner pub. We were doing a bit of drinking."

My father drank when business was bad or someone had died. "Who died?" I asked.

The Captain paused for a long time, and then began to sing. "You're my lady, I'll always love you. You're my lady." He stood, staggered for a moment, and held out his hands. "Come on, little boy, let's dance."

I stepped back from his powerful breath. He came forward, thinking that I was leading him onto the dance floor. I waited in the center of the room under the dirty chandelier. The Captain was wearing a pair of dark flannel slacks and a crisp blue shirt. I had never actually seen him in clothes other than fish-gutting overalls.

"Your father is raising you like a man. I'm going to have to talk to him about this." He laughed and coughed but stayed true to the same pattern of steps he had been dancing before. We took two steps to the left and then two steps back to the right. He led me across the floor in an oddly shaped box.

We started dancing around the room, accompanied by his mumbling. There was a knock on the hull of the ship.

"What's that?" I said.

"Probably one of those rat motherfuckers. Bessie is being hauled over to New Jersey," he sighed, and kept dancing.

I pulled back violently. "What?"

"Come on, Peanut, don't stop. I'd almost forgotten."

"Forgotten what?" I asked, pushing his hand away from my side.

The Captain walked back to the table where his jacket, flask, and cigarettes were propped. I ran outside and looked over the edge of the railing. No one was there. When I came back inside The Captain was gone. I picked up my sweatshirt and realized the extra keys to the ship were no longer in my pocket.

There was a loud knock on the hull. It sounded like a wrench slamming against hollow metal. I heard it three more times before I retreated through the kitchen.

As I began to descend the small rope ladder at the port of the ship, I repeated The Captain's words to myself and then forced them out of my thoughts. I heard the knocking again. A tugboat crew had begun to attach a web of chains to the bow of the ship. I scampered back up the rope. There were very few things that were not bolted down on the ship that I could carry. I remembered a loose stack of extra portholes hidden under a tarp near the engine room but knew that even those were too heavy to take with me. I could barely see. My usual ability to move around the ship was disturbed by panic, and I couldn't find doors that were usually unlocked.

I tried to find The Captain. Only shadows and strangers who had thrown the chains across the heavy bow looked back at me. Ropes and chains were arranged over the ship as if a dangerous criminal was being moved from one place to the next. The tiny Moran tugboat idled calmly, waiting to begin nudging the old ship away from the pier. Other ships in the harbor cut their engines for a moment and crews stood out on the decks of their own boats. After some small discussion and shoulder shrugging, she moved sadly into the current of the Hudson.

By the time I entered the local pub to look for my father, it was nine o'clock. My father was alone while a group of his friends sat at a large round table. No one looked at each other, told jokes, or smiled. I ordered a Coke from the bar and ate salted peanuts until my father noticed I was there.

"Did you see The Captain?" he asked.

I nodded as he zipped up my sweatshirt. My father slurred just a little as he spoke.

"Things are changing." He looked out over the clouds of cigar smoke and took a deep breath.

My father, William Lacey, was right, but at the time I was only thirteen, and I didn't want to hear it. The *Fulton* was being towed away, and ironically, I was losing the one place where I could imagine myself as a woman.

As I walked back toward my apartment all I wanted was a hot bath, some warm Drambuie, and a movie about men who go off to war and don't come back.

3

Ship of Fools

I rang my buzzer three times and looked around for a small stone to throw at the window. Maybe Steve thought it was one of my friends pulling off the FDR Drive after a weekend share in the Hamptons and would not answer. Sometimes the old cobblestone would flake off, and I'd find chunks of the street in front of the store. Tonight everything from Popsicle sticks to bottle caps had melted into the pools of wet tar.

A shadow moved back and forth on the ceiling of our apartment. I went down to the corner pay phone to call the apartment collect. The machine picked up and a synthetic mechanical operator cut me off before I could yell at Steve to open the door. I walked back to the doorway and put the ball of my foot on the buzzer. I held it down with my toe while I stretched my leg and counted to thirty.

A bright cherry-red truck pulled up the block. The music inside had a pallid twang that was definitely country music. It was Zoe and her fiancé. Zoe possessed the intelligence of a promising

Nobel Prize winner, but decided that doling out beer and managing her fiancé's business made her happier. It made the rest of us nervous to watch her jump on the bar and throw her bra around like a lasso. However, I was not in a position to mock her choices. It had been painfully pointed out to me on several occasions that my relationships were often the subject of conjecture among my friends.

Zoe and I had been downtown kids together. She worked for her mother in restaurants when I worked for my father on the docks. We shared circles of friends; we both knew most of the kids who had worked in their parents' restaurants or picked up their parents' distributor routes. Zoe's mother had once been a successful restaurant owner. As it always happens in New York, she had also become a failed restaurant owner. Trying to squeeze in a few marriages and some kids along the way didn't help. Zoe felt her mother treated her with the same fickleness as a demanding Manhattan crowd; sometimes she was *in* and sometimes she was *out*. Trying not to become our parents, we strove hard to make our own footprints and careers. Unfortunately we barely noticed when we'd step right into theirs.

While my father's words echoed through me, and his necessity to bark orders or rage at shipping prices became my own mantras, Zoe did the one thing every single mother screams at her child not to do: She took care of a man. She ran his business with such vigor that there was nothing left for herself when the eight-day week was done. Zoe and Aaron were the only couple I knew arguing more about wedding plans than Steve and I.

"Hey, girlie! What are you doing out here in the street with your short-shorts on?" Zoe yelled from the truck window.

"Hamptons?" I asked.

"Aaron caught a tuna! It's in the back."

"Hi, Aaron. When are you going to give up that crazy bar business and come catch fish for me?" I did my best to be friendly and civil because I liked Aaron less and less when I spent time with him.

"When women stop dancing on the bar and taking off their shirts." He smiled like a king.

I was still angry with Steve, and knew I was about to take it out on Aaron, fair or not. He was a wealthy boarding school rebel who pretended to be a redneck, local down-and-out kind of guy who had a stroke of luck building a solid bar business. To me that was worse than Steve; at least Steve never pretended to be another man. He was satisfied with his pedigree and enjoyed being an elitist. The only reason Aaron had succeeded with his bar was because of Zoe. Without her, he would have drunk his Pabst Blue Ribbon profits and harassed so many women that his place would have been burned, bombed, or bankrupt. Now it was the most popular bar in Manhattan, and one had to wait on line for an hour to take abuse from the bartenders.

When the bar first opened I had some good times, usually kissing strangers after a sweaty dance. If they peeled all the bras off the moose antlers I would find a few of my own. However, for me it was a little too redneck for New York. One night a group of men from Harlem grew tired of the flannel-shirt bigot atmosphere and charged the bouncer and the double doors. Several off-duty cops pulled out their guns. There was a long tense moment before the bouncer rose from the floor too quickly and a warning shot was fired. No one was actually hurt, and the black men backed quietly away, but the hole in the wall became a glaring reminder that night. Even in a place so ethnically mixed, New York bigotry reared its head more often then not. It was hard to be a liberal when you worked in the fish market; every skin tone had an ethnic name and a group of gross generalizations that accompanied it. After that incident at the bar I never saw Zoe the same way again, and Aaron continued to showcase his ignorance by posing as a hardheaded country boy. Aaron left his Dixie flags on the walls, but I always I wondered what his patrons would think if they knew he was a Jew.

I missed Zoe. She was a tough girl with a smart mouth and an even smarter brain to back it up. I wanted to continue loving her despite Aaron, but it was impossible. Your partner is the one to whom you tell things, things you might never say to your friends. It continued to shock and surprise me that she had chosen to share her secrets with Aaron. His jealousy, wicked temper, and disgusting social mannerisms were hard to accept, and while I might have a loud mouth and bad moods, at least I wasn't a spoiled child with a trust fund.

When they fought, Aaron came within inches of hitting Zoe. During their last argument she had sworn off him and changed the locks on her apartment. After a week of living at his mother's, Aaron promised to seek help for his drinking and temper. The engagement ring followed his humble pleas; it seemed he was committed to change. In truth he couldn't run the bar without her; he wouldn't know where to find the back bottles of bourbon or the telephone number of his own beer distributor. Zoe was his ticket to success. He had the money and she had the brains.

On occasion I would try to understand what she got out of their relationship. She would take me on a tour of her walk-in closet. Zoe had a custom collection of suede and leather pants, alligator cowboy boots, and jewelry for every fight where she had threatened to leave him. I understood this side of her and knew some of it in myself; but the things we outgrow we want our friends to overcome as well.

For the first few years I was back in Manhattan, after college, my father was strict with my salary. I found my own way to survive and dined with every horny businessman I could endure. They found my knowledge of fish "charming," and except for the occasional swarthy, saliva-ridden kiss I was saved most of the compromising indignities in exchange for a good meal. I learned quickly that unattractive men need their money to make them palatable, and I tired of them just as fast. For Zoe I knew it was the financial security. Aaron was not a prince of intellect, but he provided for her and she had money in her pocket from the moment he entered her life. After growing up with a mother teetering on the never-ending cycle of restaurant bankruptcy, no one could blame her for enjoying the success and the security.

"We're going to grill up this tuna in big steaks over at the bar tonight, thought we'd invite you and Steve." She smiled.

"I'm not sure Steve and I are on speaking terms. Could you call and invite him?" This was a dangerous ploy. Women rarely have problems announcing they are in the middle of a domestic battle, but men like to keep it a secret; they imagine no one can tell by their brooding silence.

Steve had a superiority complex, and he disliked Aaron wholeheartedly. It was strictly a case of old money versus the new kind. Aaron held up the cell phone and waved it in the air. I appreciated him for his interest in seeing a good fight and his lack of social intuition. Zoe dialed the phone and handed it to me.

"Hello, you've reached Catherine. I'm unable to come to the phone right now. Please leave a message. Wait for the beep. . . ."

"Steve? Steve honey? Steve, I'm standing outside with Zoe and Aaron and we're discussing dinner plans. Pick up the phone . . . you can't lock me out of my own apartment forever. Pick up the phone. . . ."

"I was in the shower," he lied.

"Did you cool off?"

"I doubt it," he said.

"Aaron caught a huge tuna. Would you like to go over to the bar and join them at the grill?"

"I made plans for us," he said.

"What a surprise."

"We're not an old married couple *yet*."

I looked at them and shrugged. "Steve made some plans. I'm sure it includes tearing my guest list in half and using four-letter words to practice our marriage vows."

Zoe smiled. "Not a good night for barbecue?"

"I guess not, but hey, I am *really, really* happy you came by." I took Zoe's hand and held it for a moment. I couldn't resist inspecting the back of the truck, with a quick glance, to see what Aaron caught.

"Hey! Who gut that up for you? I thought the only thing off that side of the island was shark?" I asked after noticing how clean the fillets were. It was a more delicate hand than Aaron's that had sliced them.

"We weren't exactly at the beach," said Zoe.

"Store-bought? I knew it was too clean a cut for Aaron!"

"Tell her," said Aaron.

"We were in Nevada."

"Nevada?"

Zoe held up her left hand to show me an oversize gold wedding band. It hung a little on her finger but she stretched out her hand wide so the ring rested between the webbing.

"But your engagement party is next month!" I said, forcing a laugh.

"We could barely agree on *where* to have that party. Can you imagine us trying to plan a wedding that would please my mother and his parents?" We all smiled, silently nodding our heads for a moment. "We decided it was easier to elope."

"A gutsy move from a gutsy girl," I said.

I reached into the truck cab and gave her a long hearty hug and managed to shake Aaron's hand with a genuine firmness. The hug was for strength, because I thought she would need it. The handshake was sincere because he was obviously getting the best deal of his life.

"Did you tell Emily?" I asked.

"Yes. She couldn't come tonight either."

"You didn't get married by that creepy guy who got his penis whacked off, did you?" I asked, not knowing what else to say.

"We were married by a nice old guy who looked like the lead on *The Dukes of Hazzard,*" said Aaron.

"Respectable," I said, still devastated. "Aaron, she is an amazing woman."

"I know." He smiled, that satisfied king smile that always made me want to slap the satisfaction off his face.

I wanted to say something threatening to him but didn't think it was appropriate.

Once, we were all experts at relationships. It was easier to talk, easier to understand each other, and easier to give advice without reading shelves of self-help books when we dated men we didn't expect to see again. I missed being young and stupid and thinking the dates and the tequila would last forever. Now we learned things differently, at different paces, and quite often in the hardest way possible. The more relationships I had, the more complications and questions I encountered. I wanted my relationships to be like training for a marathon. First there is excitement, then struggle, then work, then commitment, then peace. The body and the mind must trust each other and give up control. I always run faster than I am able, but if I think about how fast I am running it slows me down. I wanted a partner who could run with me without fearing when I led.

The truck pulled away, and I listened to the chorus of a song Aaron turned up on the radio: *"I like my women on the trashy side . . ."*

Galloping upstairs, two at a time, running through each thought, I burst through the door and kicked off my shoes frantically. It was a perfect way to disarm Steve. He was waiting for a full-blown-out confrontation. Before I even saw him I was on the phone.

"Emily?"

We were silent for a few seconds of considerate breathing.

Emily finally spoke: "What are we going to do?"

"I didn't think she'd do something like this," I said. "I saw the ring."

"You *saw* her?" asked Emily.

"She stopped by with Aaron. I guess they were on their way back from the airport."

"When do you think she'll tell her mother?"

"I certainly hope *before* the engagement party," I said.

"My engagement party was such a failure."

"Emily, you didn't have one."

"I had a little one. No one could come."

"Oh, yeah, that's because you put your sisters in charge and they called everyone at the last minute."

"I should have learned my lesson then and kicked them out of the bridal party."

"No kidding," I said without realizing what had just escaped from my mouth. "Emily! I'm sorry."

"You don't have sisters. It can be very complicated."

"Can we talk about that over lunch this week?"

"Definitely lunch. Try and support Zoe right now. Do the best you can."

"I'll try." I paused. "Emily?"

"Yes?"

"No one told me it was going to be so hard," I said.

"It seems like it takes a lot more time than it used to."

"You mean a lot more therapy." We both laughed for a minute.

"I'm a little confused," I said, catching Steve's eye as he sat down across from me in the bedroom.

"Call me tomorrow afternoon, and we'll pick a good time to see each other this week."

"Good. I love you, Em. Bye."

"Glad you called."

"Me, too," I said. "Me, too."

Steve glared at me. "Seems like there's a lot going on."

"Zoe eloped this weekend."

"The intelligent choice to whatever the rest of us are attempting. For once I should call Aaron and tell him that I highly respect his decision."

"I'd like to have that on tape." I stood up.

Steve reached for my arm.

"Back off," I said, and went straight into the bathroom.

Steve was right behind me. "Can't you let anyone in? I realize you must be upset about Zoe and whatever is going on between us. You haven't said two words about what happened at Emily's wedding last week, and I know you're tearing yourself apart trying to figure out what is going to happen at our own wedding." Steve put his hand on my back and helped me out of my jogging bra.

"You don't know everything that goes on in my head," I said.

"Maybe then I wouldn't have to force it out of you. We just shouldn't run together. When I'm fifty and need a knee replacement you'll be able to say the four words every man hates to hear."

"What words?"

He smiled in the mirror. "I told you so."

I wrapped my robe around my shoulders and slipped out of my running shorts. Then I sat on the toilet while Steve stood by the sink waiting for me to break down. Zoe's news was overwhelming, my fight with Steve seemed ridiculous, and now I couldn't get The Captain out of my mind.

"Do you think your parents were faithful?" I asked Steve.

"How about a bath?"

I nodded. "Do you think your parents were faithful through their whole marriage?"

"I have no doubt that my parents were faithful to one another."

Steve leaned over me on the toilet and began to run a bath. I was surprised at the extra weight gathering around his stomach. I pinched him very hard above the hip.

"Ouch."

"Tough love." I smiled.

"Why are you suddenly worried about fidelity?" he asked.

"I'd just like to know if you believe it is possible to be faithful forever."

"Do you think your parents were faithful to each other?" he asked.

When I shook my head, I noticed a small nick in the brass plating on the toilet paper holder across from me between Steve's legs. I had always loved my bathroom for having the toilet next to the shower and bath. I had a permanent table top on the toilet seat and could light a candle, read a book, drink a glass of wine, all without moving from a hot tub. Suddenly the thought of sharing it forever made me feel cramped.

"Who do you think was unfaithful, your father or your mother?"

I stood and faced him. "I think they both had affairs. They had the kind of partnership I admire, but I'm not sure it was about being in love."

"Well it would explain why Chelsea's been around all these years."

"Chelsea's our personal index. Without her, nothing would get done."

"Without her, you wouldn't have anyone to eat lunch with."

"I love Chelsea," I defended. "She's not just a convenience."

He rolled his eyes. "Look, I'm not sure marriage is always about love," he said, and sat me back down on the toilet seat and then checked the temperature of my bathwater.

"Are you checking the temperature of the bath for me because you love me?"

"Yes, but everything we do is not for love. Sometimes we do things because it looks good, or we think we should, even if we don't like it." He put his hand in the water and retrieved it quickly.

"Too hot?" I asked.

He nodded. The air was thick, and I smelled the dried sweat between my breasts. I wanted to love him with all my heart. I wanted to bury my face into his lap and enjoy the smell of his flesh. It seemed as if it would be so simple to try but my body was heavy and unwilling. Instead I could see only the increasing mass around his waist.

"A lot of long lunches?" I asked.

"More than you know."

"What do you mean?"

"We haven't had much time to talk. Our daily updates revolve around wedding itineraries, gifts we need to buy, or gifts we haven't bought."

"The only thing left on Emily's registry is *not* what I want to give her."

Steve reached into the bath, scooped a large handful of water, and then let it fall back into the tub. "I'm trying to tell you something about *my* life."

I dropped my robe and stepped into the water. It was so hot it almost blistered my calves. Steve held me around the waist while I marched from foot to foot to keep the skin from burning.

"I'll be a partner soon."

The empty enthusiasm was painful. I wrapped my hands around his waist and held him tight. Cataloging his body for my memory, he was beginning the journey as another man to pass through my life.

"I won't know for sure for another month. Every partner has asked me to lunch, cocktails, or dinner. I think we should add a few more seats for the reception."

Steve stood against me adoring my tears, believing that they were full of pride for his accomplishments.

At a cocktail party I once heard a woman discussing her numerous marriages. She laughed and threw her hair over each shoulder for effect: "Oh, him? I married him just to get rid of him." I had never quite understood how that was possible until now. It seemed easier to marry Steve and continue to entangle our lives than to attempt to untangle the intricate knot we had created as a couple.

4

Pick Up Sticks

Steve was sweet in the morning, and we almost survived without an incident, but as I finished washing our breakfast dishes he snuggled up behind me. I have spoken to a hundred women, all of whom say that the worst possible time to receive affection is when you are doing dishes. The second worst time to attempt intimacy is when I am vacuuming, and the third is when I'm folding laundry.

"Back off," I snapped.

"What is with you?"

"Steve, I hate that. My hands aren't free; I'm not in a cuddly mood. It is Monday morning and I'm in work mode and that's where I want to be." I flung off my rubber gloves and tucked in my blouse.

Most of my life I had fearlessly stuck my hand into the warm roe of dying shad and enjoyed it. Putting on rubber gloves to perform housework in order to protect my nails for the wedding was a behavior that belonged to another woman.

"If I never cuddled you, I would be a jerk who was cold and insensitive to your needs. This is classic!"

"Stop overreacting to everything!" I said in a failed attempt to be calm.

"You're screaming. All I did was give you a kiss while you were doing dishes."

"It is so belittling to have someone molest you while you are being domestic!"

He turned his back to me and walked away. "Obviously it's a feminist thing."

My hand reached for something on the counter that I hurled at Steve as he turned the corner of the doorway and entered the bedroom. It clipped him on the left shoulder, ricocheted toward the window, and smashed through it.

Steve didn't react to the thud the object made when it touched his shoulder, or the shattering sound of glass; he merely paused, took a deep breath, and collected his briefcase. He stood between me and the view of the river through the damaged window.

"By tonight either go back to being the woman who wanted to get married or I'm leaving."

I heard the bellow of my father's voice from the office downstairs. Chelsea, our secretary and oldest family friend, was trying to pacify him.

At the base of the steps that led upstairs to my apartment, he yelled: "What the hell is going on up there? Catherine, you are twenty minutes late for work, and I'm sure Steve has somewhere to go. Don't pull any crap today. I want to get some work done." His feet were climbing the stairs steadily.

Steve looked at me, then at the stairs, then back at me. "Who will be here when I get home tonight?" he asked.

I looked at the stairs, then back at Steve. I did not fear my father. I loved the cantankerous old man he was to strangers and then the quick way he bowed to my mother. My father was a catalog of dichotomies, and you rarely knew which personality was headed toward you. I learned it was easiest to ignore him, and although others saw him throwing his fists in the air in angry fits or abusive tantrums, to me he was just a little moody. I did live in fear that he would never retire and for the rest of my life I would be late for work at twenty minutes past seven. My father's feet shuffled back and forth on the mat outside my door.

Steve whispered his question again: "What should I expect tonight?"

"Catherine? Catherine? Open the door." My father knocked hard.

Looking back, I should have said something very simple like "expect to pack" and it would have all been over. Instead I kissed him lightly on the cheek and put my lips near his ear.

"Count on the woman you fell in love with." Who *that* was I had begun to wonder.

Steve kissed my forehead and reached for the door. I disappeared into the bathroom.

"Good morning, Steve."

"Good morning, Mr. Lacey."

"Where's Catherine?"

Steve was blocking his entry.

"Catherine didn't expect you to come in for work today."

My father did his best to peek inside the apartment for signs of a brawl. Steve turned to the side, allowing him to look in. I shut the bathroom door before he could see where I was hiding. As I sat in the bathroom listening to them make small talk, I wondered what had happened to my courage.

In all fairness Steve was a good person; he would raise a family, love his wife, curb lecherous thoughts toward other women, and work to uphold the American dream. I fell in love with the opportunity to belong to a country club, to be closer to my coupled friends, to sit at home and read, to have a maid, to join a parents' group, and ponder the validity of tax-deductible donations and charitable causes to fight for. I had my own fantasy of escaping the union label and living with silverware I couldn't upgrade at Sears. I now recognized that my illusions about walking away from the fish business and everything I had known were temporary. Every free moment of my life had been spent on the docks, in our delivery truck, or packing crates with ice. In my imaginary marriage to Steve I had long red nails and magazine subscriptions. It was not Steve's fault that our relationship would end. It was my fault for thinking I could be someone other than myself.

"You seem anxious, Mr. Lacey. I was on my way to work but I could make you some coffee."

"Chelsea has a full pot downstairs."

"Good, then we'll walk down together." Steve stepped into the hall and closed the door behind him.

The shadows of their feet did not move. I tiptoed to the front door, where Steve spoke in a hushed tone.

"We had a little fight, nothing much, but tension is high. Her friend from college eloped last night, and I think she's upset."

"Which one?"

"Zoe."

"The bar owner?"

"Yes."

My father liked Zoe because she could drink like a tugboat captain.

Steve spoke again. "You know Cece—she doesn't want anyone to know when she's capsizing."

My father cleared his throat and asked, "Steve? Do you think all the pressure from work is too much while she tries to plan the wedding?"

"I have my own opinion, but she is set on doing both." Steve sighed heavily.

Without the pressures of my work, at that point in the season, I could be at Steve's side when he was crowned a partner in the firm. I'd be available for dinner parties. I could stay up late, chatting with other wives, drinking sherry as a nightcap, and admiring yet another Central Park view, from yet another Fifth Avenue address.

Just a few days away from the phone at work and I would lose my stronghold as the contact in our family business. It had taken me a good three years to have people ask for me instead of my father. During those years tuna and salmon had replaced steak. Sushi evolved into an overpriced, low-fat meal that the chic paid for without questioning what they were being served. I was making a fortune keeping up with the demands of low-cal California cuisine. Fish were as much a part of my life as tying my shoes. It was disarming to people, especially in business, that a woman—a young, moderately attractive woman—knew the difference in where a fish was caught purely by its smell and the feel of its scales. Various ocean tides and waters create nuances so intricate between species that I thrived on being able to find the differences. It is like smelling flowers that grow in a California greenhouse or wild in a field. It is the difference between laundry dried in a machine or on a clothesline in a breeze. The Atlantic or Pacific creates species as opposite as the inhabitants of San Francisco and New York.

"What do you think, Steve? Is it too early for me to retire? Maybe I shouldn't pull back? Maybe I should have known better than to give her so much responsibility at this time."

"The business is just another stress on top of the wedding."

"Really? Go on." My father sounded too interested, and it bothered me.

"This argument started yesterday," said Steve.

"The fight that led to the broken window?"

"Yes."

"What happened?" A fisherman enjoys a good tale and an Irishman loves a good fight; my father delighted in both.

Steve took a deep pause, the kind of dramatic pause he uses when he practices his closing courtroom statements at home.

"Well, Catherine was beginning to fill in her December calendar. She is so overwrought with planning things that she's worried about any social events we might attend during Christmas."

"Christmas is a busy season, we usually need extra time to import any out-of-season requests," he said.

I knew that Steve was caught off guard and that my father was about to enjoy a fresh morning catch. "Of course, but she is besieged by preparation for the wedding, and managing the business makes her completely volatile and moody."

"My little Cece is trying to balance her calendar four months in advance?" asked my father with a chuckle.

"Exactly—she's overwrought."

"Or she is carefully planning ahead. If I had any doubts about Cece's ability to handle things, I'm glad to know she isn't letting the spoils of August ruin her mindset for the holiday catering season." He probably patted Steve on the shoulder, hard, and then he danced a jig on the doormat jingling the keys on his belt. "Have a good day, Steve. Thank you for this pep talk. I feel much better knowing she can take on the next thing I have in mind."

My father headed downstairs whistling a little Irish drinking song. When he reached the bottom he yelled one last thing up to

Steve. "Hey, Steve, I've thrown a few things in my lifetime, and I'm sure the longer you stay with Catherine, you will, too. For now just be glad she stopped drinking Drambuie."

When I heard Steve leave the building I went to check the damaged window. In the street he was standing among the shattered glass, delicately holding several thick chunks of crystal. I looked around the apartment to see what was missing.

"What was it?" I called down to him.

He squinted up at me. "My Waterford crystal ashtray."

"I told you smoking cigars is a nasty habit." I waved cheerfully. The look on his face told me he wasn't amused.

Overseas activity was on schedule, and I managed to arrange for a new window by six o'clock that night. My father never mentioned his talk with Steve or asked about the argument. Both my father and I had the habit of reaching for the coffeepot handle and hurling it toward the walls at the front of our office. We were quick-tempered, and the sound of shattering glass satisfied our rage.

Chelsea was quiet throughout the day. She gave me a small knowing nod when I came into work; I knew that she expected to hear all the real gossip when my father stayed home and we were in the office alone. Chelsea was originally from Dallas, Texas. She was a taffeta prom queen with big hair, big nails, and big breasts. Although she married her high school sweetheart, it didn't last long. Whenever I asked her questions about her past she said things like, "Sweetie, some parts of life are worth forgetting, and most men aren't worth talking about." I do know that she came to Manhattan years ago and was the star pupil in her secretarial school. However, she loathed the circle of men who ran the corporations she worked for. She was a meticulous typist with an insubordinate attitude, not a good combination for an executive secretary. By the time Chelsea applied to work with my family she had been fired seventeen times. My father says that during their short interview he felt as if he were being interrogated, and he figured she was tough enough to stand up to the locals.

Chelsea started a few days after we moved into the decrepit brownstone that stood across from Pier 17. The building we bought was rough and old, but my father held on fiercely to his dream. There was a small storefront where we could sell fish or open a reasonable office with a few livable rooms upstairs. Soon, the basement was stocked with special freezers, the first floor was painted sea green, and brass accessories shone in every corner. I'm sure my father had been planning for a long time to leave Brooklyn behind. My mother's father had just died, and my father was ready to improve his standard of living.

Our family was a neighborhood oddity in a place like Brooklyn. When my father and mother married I'm sure the rest of the neighborhood thought it was a perfect match. There was just one grandparent left, my parents had no living siblings, I was an only child, and there were no plans for more kids. We were loud and boisterous, but in church and at block parties we were quiet and kept to ourselves. In school I was called Creepy Catherine by kids and teachers because I preferred to work on the docks than to play hopscotch. The other kids made up stories about how I was possessed by a sea god and would someday drown myself to be closer to the fish.

When we moved to the South Street Seaport area there were no public schools in our industrial neighborhood. My mother knew I was not going to fit in a competitive uptown environment, and in an attempt to broaden my dock-learning, I was enrolled in experimental classrooms and small schoolhouses. It was hard to walk away from the behavior I had learned at my old school. I picked fights and was sent home so often that only the threat of returning to Catholic school made me embrace my alternative environment. When I was willing to sign a contract promising that I'd sit in the "circle of need," "share," and "stop punching," I was allowed to return to school.

In my mind, school was just an interruption to working summers. My only sense of peace came from hauling crates and smelling the aroma of sweaty rubber slickers. Historic barges and buoys were the things that grounded me.

My parents had insisted that I be who I wanted to be without bowing to my sex. My mother, Jane, was not feminine, but she was attractive and strong. My father could be hard and defensive, but he was also tender and vain, and he hated if he lost a strand of the cherished salty white hair on his head. He was often more concerned with my brawny, boyish appearance than was my mother, who preferred musk scents and shopping in the men's department.

Their wardrobes were not extensive, but they were timeless, like an old bank. As a child Jane had worn church hand-me-downs, and most of her clothes came from boys on the block. She had learned how to wear men's clothing with aplomb. Instead of jewelry she liked the flexibility of a quality scarf with her suit. Financial success gave them some room for indulgences. My father obsessed over watches, and my mother bought shoes—but they both still wore traditional, conservative suits. Chelsea was the only person in our office who wore skirts.

By the time I graduated from college my mother was a pro at knowing which, out of hundreds of blue suits on a rack, would best fit a woman's body. She liked a small men's shop in midtown where they tailored the suits to fit and bought quality fabrics from Italian mills. Mr. Carlton had helped my mother and father for over ten years. Though a few of the newer salesmen balked at us when we arrived, Mr. Carlton was ready to help a second generation of Lacey women.

"Catherine, try these and we'll take the three that look the best."

I looked at my father, then back at my mother. "Is three enough?" I asked.

"Three is fine. Suits are like bras; you only need a few to start with. Besides, it doesn't include shoes." My mother smiled.

My mother had brought one pair of midsize pumps for me to wear while I tried the suits on. It was early when we arrived, but by the time I was on my way to the dressing room I noticed a crowd of older men milling around with their sons.

"Excuse me, but may I ask what are you doing here?" asked a freckled young man in the crowded dressing room.

"Following in my mother's footsteps," I said, annoyed.

"Don't they have suit stores for girls?" questioned another.

"Women," I said.

"Don't you think you might look like a, you know, a guy or something in a men's suit?" Someone commented toward the back of the room.

"Don't worry, I work in the fish market so I'll always smell like a bitch!" I stormed out of the dressing compartment without a shirt underneath my suit, exposing the heart on my lavender bra. Mr. Carlton rolled his eyes and the tailor sighed. My father ignored us and continued to look at ties. My mother embraced me, placed an arm around my waist, and trailed her fingers lightly over my furrowed brow and cinched lips.

"You are a very handsome woman. The right person will adore you for it."

For twenty-nine years I was happy wearing suits, working on the docks, having sex for fun, and challenging the rules of what defined women, but somewhere in the last year I had begun to convince myself that only a wedding dress would make me feminine. There is a time that being a tomboy is acceptable. When you are young it is cute, tolerated, humorous, or builds personality.

The moment Janice Maloney stopped wearing her brother's baseball shirts I knew I was alone. I saw Janice from across the street, holding several books under her exploding breasts in a low-cut peach sweater that showed the frilly edge of her polyester training bra. Janice Maloney walked by me on our way to recess with just a quick wave as she went to share lipsticks with a few other girls on the bench. I was the only one left on the stickball team that tied my hair back and stuck it under my cap.

Steve filled me with the false expectation that if I managed to stay with him long enough, we would marry, but squeezing myself into a wedding dress was as uncharacteristic as giving up my well-earned position as shortstop and trading it in for Janice Maloney's training bra. This morning's confrontation made me realize that if I didn't learn how to accept myself now, when it mattered most for me to define who I really was, I would surely marry and spend my life trying to be the wrong person.

5

The Whole Truth

Chelsea called out to me on the intercom, "Have a minute?"

"For you? Always."

"No. For your father."

"You tricked me," I said.

"He'd like to see you when he gets back from lunch."

"He's out now?"

"Until three-thirty."

"Do you want to know what happened?" I asked.

"I already read it on page six of the *Daily*'s gossip column."

"Really? I'm flattered."

"Not you! I read about Zoe."

If her elopement had already leaked to the gossip section of the paper, I imagined that their small barbecue had turned into a riotous beer bash.

"I hope Zoe's mother reads the *Times*," I said.

"Have you spoken to her yet?" asked Chelsea.

"She stopped by last night, but I wasn't in the mood to be supportive."

"That doesn't seem like the only thing you're upset about," she said, appearing at my door.

I pushed myself back from the desk. "Why? Did you see any unidentifiable flying objects this morning?" I smiled.

"Nothing I haven't seen in this office before."

I looked at the sun sending light through Chelsea's hair; it had a gold-and-purple halo. The naked eye couldn't see it, but I had grown accustomed to watching for small changes in her hair color.

"Is it Emperor Tang? Part of the sturgeon fish family?" I asked.

"Good call. Your father was way off. He said yellow-striped emerald triggerfish." She smiled.

"Way too much purple for a triggerfish, although you could take it as a compliment because it's known for its hardiness and aggressive nature."

She sat in the soft suede chair across from my desk. "So? Tell me."

"Everything Steve says makes me angry. I want to fight with him even when I don't really care."

"You never argued with the loony boyfriends." Chelsea gave me a funny look and then started to laugh. I'm sure she was thinking about the three weeks I wore turtlenecks until the color of the beet juice subsided. "Maybe you love Steve because he doesn't let you get away with things."

I reached for one of Chelsea's cigarettes. "Want to join me?"

Chelsea opened her fingers to accept one from me. "You're smoking?"

"Today seems like a perfect day to start."

We both watched the smoke curl around the ceiling and then slip into the air conditioner like a snake being charmed into its basket.

"Cece, baby, stop wearing the martyr party hat." There was bright-red lipstick on the end of her cigarette.

Even though both women were in their sixties, my mother's gray suits and pageboy hair seemed dull compared to Chelsea's sexy heels and bright accessories. I wondered if Steve was right about Chelsea and my father. Chelsea was still attractive and would be till they laid her in a coffin.

Chelsea finished her cigarette. "You have choices."

"Do we?" After a long silence I asked, "My father's retirement has nothing to do with proving I can run the business, does it?"

She nodded. "When you really want the business to be yours I know the old man is ready to move on. They worry that once they are both in retirement you'll push me out with fancy computers or someone younger."

"As if you can't type six times as fast as I can. Besides, who would keep the computers running?" I thought about the delicate balance of information in a small business so tightly woven to your skin that it is hard to strip yourself of it at the end of the day.

"Do you want to stay?" I asked quietly, like a scolded child.

"Working for you alone will be a lot more fun than working for your father. Maybe your mother would come back to work and we could be the three musketeers in skirts."

"You're the only one who wears skirts."

Chelsea smiled with half her mouth and cocked her head to the side. She looked like a singer for a country western band. She kissed me on the forehead and held my chin in her hands. "You are fine, take your time, but be honest—*especially*—with your-self."

"I don't know if I want to marry Steve."

"That's a good first step. We'll work on the rest later." Chelsea winked at me.

"What?" I asked coyly.

"Things you should forgive about your parents."

I sat back in my chair and laughed as she sauntered out the door.

I called Steve to see when we could talk. Once I had made up my mind, I needed to act on it before I lost my nerve.

"Steve Montgomery, Scudder, Scadden, Skipowitz and Dawn," he answered.

"Where's your secretary?" I asked.

"Under my desk."

I was struck by the acute possibility that she might be.

"Have you had lunch?"

"No," he said.

"Order something for us and I'll jump on the train," I said.

"What's the hurry?" he asked.

"I think we should talk."

"Can't it wait until the end of the day?"

"I just need to see you," I said.

I wanted to watch him eat an oversize midtown deli sandwich, in his suit, sitting at his large desk, and drinking diet soda. I knew that image would fill me with enough disgust and courage to ter-minate our engagement. Just as I was out the door Susan called from San Francisco.

"Hey, you were on my list of people to talk to today," I said.

"Good, but can we save it until Friday?"

"I suppose."

"I fly home tonight, and I'm out of my mind with things to do. By the way, can you show Tanya around the city on Friday?"

"Tanya? The lesbian?"

"No, that's Brittany, the rich one who lives in Chicago. Tanya is my friend from California. We're teachers at the same school," she said.

"Right, right. Sorry."

"We'll take the train to the city and a cab down to the seaport."

"OK."

"Are you sitting down?" she asked.

"I'm on my way out the door." I looked at my watch.

"Jeannine's engaged! We're going to have a barbecue or something on Saturday."

"Your sister's engaged?" Susan's wedding next weekend would be an extension of a serious celebration. "What made Enrique finally ask?"

"Five years isn't enough time to think it over?"

"Five years already? I remember when they started sleeping together on my sofa. I paused. "Look, I really need to talk to you."

"What is it? Trouble in paradise?" she asked.

"The ship is sinking," I said.

"We can find you someone else."

"What?"

"Steve's a good guy, but he doesn't have a clue as to who you are."

"How can you say that? I thought you liked him!"

"I liked him because I want you to get pregnant at the same

time as me so our kids can grow up together. Anyway, he has fat legs. You don't want kids with fat legs." She laughed.

"I wish you'd told me sooner," I mumbled.

"Who can ever tell you anything you don't want to hear? I just hoped for a kid."

"I wish I didn't buy the dress."

"You'll use it."

"Easy for you to say. You're pretty sure you will get married next week."

"I love you, Cece. There is one just for you."

"Of course," I said. "I just need to find him."

On the subway uptown I managed to sit in the only car with no air-conditioning. I thought about my brief conversation with Susan; it was just like her to tolerate Steve purely because he enhanced the plan she designed for our lives. She and I had met during a summer program for international business. It was a four-week program offered by the United Nations that covered cultural diversity and the global economy. Susan wanted to get into politics, and my father thought I should understand the world beyond the seaport. Unfortunately, the program was geared toward graduate students. Susan and I were the only ones under thirty.

There was a television set in the smoking lounge of the educational wing at the United Nations. Susan would burst through the doors at three o'clock and turn on *General Hospital.* By the end of a lecture on cultural awareness, American infiltration in former Communist markets, or religious tolerance, I craved nicotine.

We sat separately at first. I stared out the window, and she stared at the television. We shared some pretzels from the vending machine, and then we took turns buying each other sodas. The next day I brought snacks from home, and she filled me in on the back story to the soap. Together we fought off young administrators who wanted to change the channel and instead allied ourselves with the secretaries on break. Our final project was based on the importance of using American culture to educate overseas markets. Susan and I played videotapes of *General Hospital* to explain the best way to infiltrate the economic systems of evolving nations. While other students scoffed at us, the professor praised our insight and agreed that most supply-and-demand fluctuations occur due to a dramatic rise in pop culture exchanges. After that we were free to do what we wanted without too much criticism.

Susan was from a small town in Pennsylvania, so we spent the next few years commuting between Grand Central and Trenton Train Station. At her house we would wash her car, weed her mother's garden, or help her father rake leaves. A weekend at Susan's meant we were roused early on Saturday morning to study for school, and a balanced breakfast waited for us on the table. On Sundays her family brought me to their Quaker meetinghouse. During meditation I began to hear the noises the earth made as it moved through each season. Branches broke from the trees in the winter under the weight of the snow and ice. The brittle snap echoed through the congregation. The soft smell of earth and forsythia came through the windows in the spring by comparison to the sound of construction that marked the change of season in Manhattan.

When the simplicity of Susan's life became overbearing, she would escape to see me in the city. We'd sneak into nightclubs and go drinking at places where they never questioned our age. We pretended to be secretaries or dental hygienists. I had no cur-

few and kept a stocked dingy prewar kitchenette on the third
floor. We came home late and stayed up until the morning eating
food we bought at all-night supermarkets. I needed Susan's sanity
to reel me in when no one else was watching and she needed my
wildness to help her experience life before settling down. Susan
taught me how to spend a quiet evening at home without going
insane. Jeannine, now newly engaged, had the same soothing
quality.

It was on a hot city day like this one that Jeannine and I
learned we could live together. When she was between apartments she stayed with me. At the time I was *still* in the old attic
room on the third floor of our office building. Jeannine and I
would rush into the apartment almost screaming with disgust at
touching a sticky subway banister. In my mind, fish guts were
clean, blood was pure, but a subway banister was plagued with
disease. We both hated dirty feet under the covers and wearing
shoes in the apartment. On Sunday nights we had a standing date
to order in food and watch old movies. Having that time together
allowed us to become friends independently of my close relationship with her sister. For me it meant having two guardian angels,
and when they relocated to California I missed them desperately.

In between stations the subway came to a halt and the lights
went out. I waited for an announcement, but there was nothing.
Although I had been deep within my own thoughts, I had noticed
that a good-looking businessman sat next to me.

"Do you have a cellular phone I could use?" I asked.

"Be my guest, but we're in a tunnel. Not a chance you'll get
through."

"It will be a cheap call then," I laughed, and wiped the sweat
from my lip.

The conductor announced that the excessive heat had caused electrical problems, and after twenty minutes of waiting a station manager suggested we remove any extra layers of clothing to prevent heat exhaustion.

"What do you think that means?" I asked out loud.

"I think it means 'Don't panic, but it will be a few hours.' "

In the shadows of the tunnel as he stripped off his suit jacket I held his briefcase. Fumbling in the dark, to help me out of my jacket, the palm of his hand touched my shoulder. I felt a familiar tingle of attraction run rapidly through me.

"Married?" I asked him.

"Separated. You?"

"Engaged."

"The trouble with engagements is they always lead to marriages." He opened his briefcase. I heard papers fall out onto his lap. Holding my wrist with one hand he slipped a manila folder into it. "It makes a good fan," he said.

"We can take turns?" I offered, and fanned him for a moment.

Our knees pressed against each other slightly harder than they had before. We made no effort to separate ourselves even when our forearms became sticky. Other people complained loudly and stumbled around the subway car in the dark, but we were ironically content. The shadows and the heat would have been terrifying without him but I enjoyed the quiet between us. He knew nothing about me, and I liked imagining he was perfect and so was I.

After an excruciating hour of resisting I placed my head on his shoulder.

"Are we thinking about the same things?" he asked.

"I'm sure," I said.

"Do you sneak around?" he asked in a hushed voice.

"Not yet."

"Don't start. It becomes easier every time." I sat up and rested my head against the plastic curve of the seat. "I didn't mean you had to move," he said.

"I just don't want to make it worse."

"Of course."

"I'm having a hard enough time right now."

"Wedding jitters?"

"It seems a bit more serious than that."

"Do you love him?"

"Did you love her?" I asked back.

"I wasn't accusing. Just asking."

"I was on my way now for one good look at him before I broke off our engagement." I sighed and laughed a little at the thought of Steve eating *two* sandwiches.

"Wedding jitters happen to everyone. You're not alone."

"It didn't happen to my friends," I said.

"It happened to mine."

"You're a guy—guys never want to get married."

"That isn't true. We want to get married and have children. Being a father is an important step for us, but we get a lot of messages that say it's the end of our life." He sighed a little.

"Is it?" I asked.

"No, but divorce isn't either."

"What was wrong with your marriage?" I asked.

"Are you a therapist?"

"Far from it."

He laughed. "Marriage compounds problems you already had, but you want to believe it can fix them. In the beginning of a relationship a man always tells a woman who he is, but the woman doesn't hear him. Men tell you everything you need to know to get along with them."

"What did you tell your wife that she didn't hear?" I asked.

"That I'd cheat. My father was a womanizer. There were seven boys in the family and the only time I was special was when a woman noticed me."

"You told her you would chase other women?"

"I *warned* her."

"She chose not to believe you?" I asked.

"She believed that once I was married it wouldn't be so important to me anymore."

"Are you confident you were really straight with her?"

"Blunt."

"Are you Catholic?" I asked.

"Why?"

"I was raised a Catholic and either you go for guilt or not. I'm sure she figured that guilt would keep you from fooling around."

"But I just spend more time at confession," he said. "Why did you think I was Catholic?"

"Seven brothers."

"How many siblings do you have?" he asked.

"None," I laughed nervously.

"Weirdo," he said.

"Do you still go to confession?" I asked.

"When I've got good stories and I think Father Connelly is bored by all the bingo swindlers."

"Does everyone confess to a *Father Connelly?*"

"You had one, too?"

"Oh, yeah. And a Sister Mary Margaret."

We were quiet for some time after that. People were listening to our conversation. Beggars had gone through each car twice and collected something from almost every passenger by threatening to touch him or her in the dark. A woman in a connecting car fainted and a few people called out for a doctor, but I thought only of the man next to me. I imagined our life together, my stranger and me: our kids, a house, a place where I could read a book in the sun and drink wine in the afternoons.

A fan went on and the lights flickered. The train had several loud false starts and then stopped again. The passengers cheered and groaned. I believed everyone would be happy to move except for us.

"I'll be sorry when it's over," I said.

The stranger put his hand on my knee, and I felt the warmth of his palm through my pants.

"Me, too," he said.

"When we arrive at the next stop I need to get back downtown," I sighed.

"I thought you were coming with me," he chuckled.

"I think it was important to meet you," I said.

I could feel him looking at me in the darkness of the train.

Sensuously, he said, "Good luck figuring it out."

"Is luck all we have?" I asked.

We laughed uncomfortably for a moment, and then I moved slightly forward to search for his cheek. He met me with his lips and pulled me toward him. When we separated I realized that I recognized the taste of his lips. I gasped—this man wasn't a complete stranger. I had finally found Johnny McDougal.

Just then the train lurched forward and the lights went on. I was too stunned to say anything, and as we stood up Johnny slowly stuffed the envelopes we had used for fans back into his briefcase. Only his freckles had faded and he seemed content just to smile at me. We waited in the crowd by the door.

"I've got a few more stops," he said, and then handed me one of his business cards. "Just in case you want to call."

I nodded.

He squeezed my hand good-bye as I shuffled through the explosive rowdy group of frustrated New Yorkers to the platform. Still stunned, I turned to look at him again until the doors closed.

As the train pulled away, in the dense herd of commuters, I saw him lunge forward against the doors and mouth the question: *"Catherine?"*

6

Speak Now

By the time I was twelve Jonathan McDougal let me touch his penis behind the alley at the soda shop. Johnny was thirteen or fourteen. He had a job sweeping up at the Candy Corner, a local hamburger shop with candy and some toiletries. He looked important with his crisp white shirt, blue striped apron, and dark, new jeans. All the boys who worked for Mr. McMillan wore the uniform, but he was the one who stood out. I suppose if McMillan wasn't so fond of room-temperature Scotch or busy with the widow, Mrs. Santiago, he might have noticed that Johnny disappeared from the sales counter for long bouts of time.

Johnny was the cutest thing I'd ever seen. He had a pug nose and freckles scattered across his forehead. What we learned from each other was punishable by the Devil's wrath and enough Hail Marys to keep us praying until we were twenty. At the time, I was sure I was the only girl who knew he had a little bit of hair that felt like feathers between his legs.

I had seen pictures of what people did to make babies, and

though I knew I was missing some parts, I wanted to see what it felt like.

"No," said Johnny, "we have to be married."

"I want to try it."

"I don't think it'll work."

"I don't care. I want to."

"What if we get caught? Are you sure?"

"Double sure," I said with confidence, putting my lips on his.

They were thinner than I thought they would be and I moved my head from side to side like they did in the movies. I kept my hand moving up and down on his pants to feel the changes in his penis.

He let out a small moan. "Does it hurt?" I asked.

"No, it feels good."

"Why are you moaning then?"

"I don't know."

As things became more intense we looked up and down the alley and decided we could go behind the garbage cans for more privacy.

"Wait," said Johnny. While I stood in the alley he sneaked inside and came back with a fresh, clean red-and-white-check tablecloth from the stockroom. We crawled between the garbage cans and spread the cloth down on the ground. Johnny lay on his back and lifted the bottom of his apron. In the storeroom light I could see the creamy skin on his stomach. The tip of his elastic white underwear showed at the top of his pants when he undid his belt.

"I think I'm supposed to lie down on top of you," he said.

"I know, but I saw it in a magazine where she was on him."

"Maybe we shouldn't."

"Are you chicken?" I asked.

"No."

"Good—because I wouldn't do it with a chicken," I laughed, kissing Johnny hard on the lips.

"Take them off," I ordered playfully.

"You first."

I stood straight up and pushed my panties down around my brown suede saddle shoes without bending my knees.

"Now you," I ordered again.

"Maybe we can do it if I pull it out."

"No. Take them off."

"I'm the one who is supposed to tell you what to do."

"Why?"

"I don't know—it's what my brother says."

"Take them off or I'm going," I said.

Johnny seemed to panic at the thought of my leaving. Looking back it seemed funny that the way I ordered him around was the same way I would push the girls on the playground and tell them what to do when they played on my dodgeball team.

"Can I just push them down a little?" he asked politely.

"I guess."

He wriggled his jeans and briefs down his thighs, which made his legs stick straight out as if they were tied together at the knees. Having heard the guys at the docks and the fish market talk about sex, I figured if I put his penis inside me I would suddenly form huge breasts and curly pubic hair like a scene from *The Incredible Hulk.* I got on my knees and lowered myself down over him. He closed his eyes.

"What does it feel like?"

"Kind of tight."

"Does it feel good?"

"I think so. It feels different."

I was already bored and decided to squat on my heels to keep my knees from getting sore.

"Oooh," he said.

"Does it hurt?"

"No, no, ooh."

Johnny grabbed me by the waist and started moving me around on top of him.

"This is dumb," I said, but it wasn't over for Johnny. He started shaking, and I thought he was getting sick. "Don't throw up." I put my hand over his mouth.

He pushed his tongue on my finger and shuddered again. His eyes flew open and then closed.

"Can we do it again sometime?" he asked.

"Yeah, but don't scare me and make those faces, OK?"

"Sorry."

"Do you feel good?" I asked.

"Yeah, kind of funny though, a little nauseous, like I just took a roller-coaster ride."

I stood up and watched his penis shrink.

"Next time I want to feel good, too," I said.

"I think it's easier for guys."

"I'll get a book or something," I said, and pulled up my panties, which were wrapped around my left ankle.

I pushed the garbage cans aside to look for my books in the dark, when Johnny came up behind me and put his hands over my eyes.

"Are you going to tell?" he asked.

"Who?" I asked. "Father Connelly?"

"I don't know."

"If you breathe a word to anyone, especially your stupid brothers, I'll make sure they put you in a psycho school for forcing me to touch you in the alley," I said. "Next time I want to feel good. We look at the book. Got it?"

"Yeah," he said, and gave me a quick kiss on the cheek.

I had a year experimenting with Johnny that no one ever knew about. From the outside it looked like he had adopted me as his kid sister. My mother eagerly drove us to roller-skating rinks, parks, movies, and allowed him to sleep over on weekdays. It was long before the age that it could have even occurred to my parents that he and I knew what sex was. It would be years before I understood they knew more than I suspected. My father adored him, and I suppose Johnny needed the paternal attention. In my house he was special. My parents lavished him with candy, food, and games. My grandfather liked to play cards with him and rehash grotesque war stories about men losing limbs, blood, and women.

Johnny and I finally found a book that showed us what was supposed to make a woman feel good. There were quotes from all different women about things they liked and photos of a vagina.

"It looks kind of scary," said Johnny.

"Yeah, it does."

I had to admit he was right. It looked wrinkled and sad. I had such a tiny little area that was going to make me feel good and his was always expanding. Looking at the pictures I wished I could be a boy instead.

"I like you as a girl. If you were a boy I don't think we'd get to do this stuff."

"But we'd have more time."

"What do you mean?" he asked.

"You know, *stupid.*"

"No, I don't know, *stupid.*"

"Once I get the thing every month I have to stop having sex until I want one."

"When will you get it?"

"Do you even know what the *thing* is?"

He nodded. "We could make babies," he said cheerfully. As Catholic kids we felt this was part of our destiny.

We both returned to inspecting the photos slowly and pointing at italicized words we didn't understand. In less than three months we had a comfortable working vocabulary of sexual terms.

I would say: "How does it feel when I touch your penis?"

He would ask: "Am I rubbing your clitoris too hard?"

Though neither of us knew it at the time, we were way beyond what Health class would ever attempt to teach us, especially in a religious environment. For my thirteenth birthday Johnny said he had a surprise for me. I couldn't wait to open my gifts. There was a diary from him, it was pretty and had flowers on it, but I was disappointed. My parents didn't even think twice when I asked if he could stay over.

That night when he came to bed I pushed him out. "Where's my surprise?"

"You have to touch me to see it."

"I'm tired of that," I said.

"This time it will be different."

I began the same stroking pattern we always used. First slow, and then fast, then slow and very fast at the end. This time when the waves of his orgasm occurred he ejaculated for the first time in my hand. He moaned and rolled onto his back for a moment.

He leaned up on one arm and whispered: "I had this dream a few nights ago. We were having sex in the alley behind McMillan's, and then you turned into the widow Santiago. When I woke up I had stuff all over my sheets."

I started to cry softly.

"What's wrong? I thought you'd be happy," he said.

"*You* can make babies but I *can't* yet."

"I'll wait for you."

"It would be nice," I said to make him sleep, and he did, forgetting for the first time to give me a small kiss or a touch on the arm.

It was only a few days later that he graduated from middle school and stopped coming to see me. For months afterwards, I slept with the last remainder I had of him tucked under my pillow. Somewhere in a trunk of fish skeletons, shark teeth, and nautical paraphernalia there is a white vinyl belt with characters from the *Peanuts* gang embroidered on it.

After Johnny left it became important for me to be "the number one son"; we all missed him. My mother had complications when I was born and said she could never have another child. It would be years before I learned that was a lie. She didn't want any more children, but in our neighborhood it was easier to say she was unable to get pregnant. She was a woman other people called *hard*. After her father died she protected herself from loss by turning a shoulder to most things—even my birth did not soften her. In fact, at times, I believe it made her coldhearted. She was always preparing for my death, or trying to prepare me for hers. My mother taught me two things: how to wear a suit and how to be independent.

I locked Johnny's business card in the company safe, drank two short glasses of Drambuie and half a bottle of wine by the time Steve called to say he wasn't coming home.

"We have a new window," I said apologetically.

"I really need to concentrate on this case. I'm going to have to fly down to Florida next weekend to meet with the chairman of the company."

"Next weekend is Susan's wedding."

Silence. "I'm sorry," he said.

"Me, too."

"I didn't do it on purpose."

"Just coincidence," I said, pouring another glass of wine, wondering if Johnny needed a drink as badly as I did tonight.

"Before you get too drunk to reason with, I also made plans with one of the partners for this weekend."

"Why don't you marry a partner? Then you won't have to come home to get fucked, you can just stay at the office and take it up the ass."

I hung up, drank the rest of the wine, ate a bowl of popcorn, and fell asleep on the couch.

The next day I stumbled around the office hiding my puffy eyes. Steve never called and my father barked out orders that kept us all busy until it was close to cocktail time. It was a bad day for Mickey Little to drop by and argue prices, and as always, he arrived without an appointment.

"Mickey Little is here, and he wants to speak with you," Chelsea said with traceable annoyance. She was never fond of him.

"Cece, I'm in the neighborhood and we need to talk about those flat fillets you overcharge me for." He barged in the office without waiting for an answer. I did not stand to greet him.

"Can I get a cup of coffee?" he asked.

"Mickey, you can get a better cup of coffee in any bistro you own."

"You can't move your ass to get me a coffee, but it's easy for you to charge me nine bucks a pound?"

"My shipments come with a guarantee. Find someone else who will suck up the costs if it turns bad before the set date."

"You're clever, but you're overpriced and everyone knows it."

I knew better than to engage him in conversation, but at the same time I couldn't help myself. "Who's everyone?"

"Those slanted-eye bastards are talking."

"Do you mean people of Asian descent?"

"No, but the Chinks are fed up, too."

"Would that be Thailand Chinks, Hong Kong Chinks, Burmese Chinks, Vietnamese Chinks, Cambodian Chinks, or Tibetan Chinks?"

Mickey pulled uncomfortably at one of his gold chains. He was one of the few men in the world who could wear gold chains. He went to the gym every day, waxed his chest hair, and he had the same smooth olive skin since puberty. In the summers, when his family went to Italy for the month of August, he would come back with rich chestnut-colored skin.

"We all got the fever, Cece. Tuna's hot now, and next week the big bloody bitch will be traded in for ostrich. You just watch your back and drop your prices."

Exasperated by the banter, I called his bluff. "Buy from someone else if it would make you feel like you saved a buck. Honestly, though, if I were in your position, I'd be pretty careful about pissing off your clientele. They don't understand disappointment."

Mickey's restaurant drew in the chic and the young Mafia. When you sat in his restaurant it was like being in the middle of a

European fashion magazine. Everything was glossy, brightly colored, and curtained by cigarette smoke.

"You know what I don't like about you?"

"Me personally, Mickey, or my prices?"

"Both. Don't you want to know?"

"No, but I think you'll tell me regardless—"

Mickey cut me off. "That's it! It's that princess crap you always pull. You smell like fish, but you sit around in your pretty office pretending you're better than the guy standing by his ice block."

I nodded.

"You walk around with your fancy pens and pretend like you didn't suck face and smoke cigarettes with the rest of us."

Mickey was angry we never had sex. I had been on the other side of his wrath since we were fifteen after playing a game of Seven Minutes in the Cooler. He was too forceful with his tongue, and I let him know it by biting down. Even virgin Italian lovers do not like to be critiqued. Although his father was a client of my father's, I would have never secured Mickey's attention if I had opened my legs to him. It is a fine line with certain men. I flirted with him because it gave me more power. Every waitress who worked for him knew that screwing him in the basement stockroom was a job requirement. It was painful for Mickey's ego that I, being one of the less pretty, and more unglamorous, women in his life never gave in to his overtures. I put my hand over Mickey's.

"Eight and a quarter and you stop side orders to Fo Tang Sturgeon Company."

"Yeah, good, *and?*" He raised an eyebrow.

"I'm too old to do business that way."

"Cece, you aren't a supermodel, but I know you like doing it. Those skinny broads just lay there. I mean you'd think it's perfect: They don't want anything, they never make you wait—but man, they don't move. I can't believe I'd rather have my way with your soft freckled ass!"

I couldn't help but laugh. Mickey's charm was in his boyish bluntness. Mickey was the worst kind of man a woman could marry if she cared about fidelity, but the best kind of man if she cared about loyalty.

"Mickey, if my wedding doesn't work out, maybe you can do some pinch-hitting."

"What? Mr. Uptown isn't perfect even with all those white teeth?"

"Actually, no, Mickey—I think the whole thing is over."

"Come on. What's the problem?"

"I don't like the way he smells."

The two of us broke into hysterical laughter. Nothing seemed more ironic to the owner of a fish wholesaler and an Italian restaurateur. I walked him to the street door.

"Eight and a quarter and no side buys." I held out my hand to shake on it.

"Call if you need me, Cece."

"If I need you, I'll just stop by."

Mickey kissed my hand and we nodded our heads, the both of us remembering that the last time he made a pass at me we were in our early twenties. I had reeled away so swiftly in my fury, that I knocked over three crates of eggplants. As my hands slipped over each round bulb and firm green nipple from the vine, I was deeply aroused. If it had been any other man *but* Mickey I would have enjoyed the lush purple eggplants rolling around underneath me as we had sex.

*   *   *

When I locked the doors and turned on the answering machine, my father accosted me in the foyer.

"Catherine, we need to have a meeting before next Monday. I know you were trapped on the subway yesterday, but I've planned some things you should know about," he said.

"It can wait until next week, Dad."

Chelsea spun around on her heels and looked at me. My father was frozen. In all the years we had worked together I had cursed at him, and yelled at him, thrown things at him, but never, ever, had I at any time suggested he wait.

"*What?*"

"It can *wait* until next week. If all our deliveries are on schedule, everything else is unimportant." I looked directly into my father's eyes.

Exhausted by the strain of the summer heat and my lingering memories of Johnny, I had no energy left to listen to him. My father began to raise his scrawny finger to scold me, but instead he pointed it at Chelsea. It was as if he knew that pointing it in my direction would be a disaster.

"I don't know what you ladies are cooking up, but I don't like it."

Gently I took my father's finger in my hand. The bones under his thin leathery skin were swelling with arthritis between the joints. I stood there silently, holding his index finger and decided it was my business. I was finished working for him. I can still feel his creaking joints in my enclosed palm and how my pulse quickened and then grew steady as I stared him down.

"We don't need you for the rest of the week," I said without letting his finger go.

"You're in control then?" He nodded slowly as if taking in a badly told joke.

"Yes, I am."

"When can we have a meeting?"

"Next week." I smiled encouragingly and reluctantly let go of his finger.

For him and me this was either the end of an era or the beginning of a long cold war. I turned my back on them and retreated into my office.

Chelsea knocked on the door when he was gone and offered me a cigarette.

"Looks like it was another long night," she said.

"One of the first that I've spent alone in a long time."

"What happened yesterday on the subway train?"

"I was given a sign not to marry Steve, and I drank a few short ones after work, and then I drank an entire bottle of wine trying to forget I was engaged."

Chelsea walked around my desk and took my hand. "I'm sure you're not the only one. Why don't you go on up to sleep now and try to stay away from the booze."

By the time I set the office alarm I was exhausted by the day's events and barely able to climb the stairs. Chelsea went home shaking her head and mumbling that she had to call my mother. I never turned the lights on in my apartment, and I listened to the summer traffic go by until I fell asleep. Late in the evening I woke up and checked my messages. One was from Emily confirming lunch plans for Thursday. The other was from Basswinder, the English estate where we had booked our wedding. Basswinder called to say they would retain the deposit fee if we canceled the wedding at least ninety days in advance. It was information *I* had not requested. I wanted to be angry or at least feel cheated that *he* had called to investigate what it would cost to cancel our wedding, but honestly I thought losing the twenty-thousand-dollar deposit fee cheaper than a divorce. Sleep came easier after that.

On Wednesday, I waited in a pair of Steve's pajamas for Chelsea to arrive.

"What are you doing?" she asked when she unlocked the door and found me on the stairs.

"I'm contemplating whether or not I'm going to give Steve back these pajamas with all his other crap." I spilled a little coffee in my lap.

Chelsea sat down beside me. "Cigarette? I think it's too early for a drink." She opened her silver holder.

"I quit." I took one from the case.

"Your mother is coming in for lunch today."

"Don't you think I need to work up to family visits?" I hung my head between my legs and exhaled into my coffee cup.

"After your performance yesterday I think you're doing fine."

"Do you think he'll come back to the office today?" I asked.

She smiled. "His appointment is next week."

"I can't really afford it, but I need to stay in bed. This is officially the first day I work for myself and I'm taking it off. If we forward all the calls upstairs, you can watch soap operas and I can cry."

"Sorry, pumpkin, but I think we have something on the books."

"I have a meeting next week with a new restaurant owner and a few of the 'conceptual' consultant junkies." I should prep for it I thought; then I decided I'd prefer to wallow.

"What about the Mendoza account?"

"What do they need?" I asked.

"Jumbo shrimp for a private party."

"This is one of Dad's small-time hustles, isn't it?" I asked.

"You know how many restaurants they own out on the island." Chelsea winked.

"I suppose the shrimp is a gift?" I asked.

Chelsea sighed and nodded.

"Call Rocco, use the Fish Exchange, tell them to deliver three hundred jumbo, steamed and deveined. Tell him to put it on clean, shaved ice and send me the bill. We'll use one of my inspection notices to show a defunct product and write it off."

"What about a gift or donation?"

"I don't think the Mendozas pay taxes, much less have any not-for-profit organizations," I said.

"It's a christening. I'm sure a priest will be there."

Chelsea knew I hated using my fish inspection notices unless it was an emergency. I had taken a long tedious course so I could verify the freshness of my own fish like the government inspectors. I spent three months at a camp in Maine smelling the bellies of rotting fish and listening to a room full of men make jokes about women. When we needed to provide large gifts to families like the Mendozas, I allowed myself to deduct several shipments a year as tax losses. I had been frugal with my inspection reports thus far because I wanted to write off some oysters, tuna, and salmon for my own wedding.

"Find out if Rocco could deliver the shrimp to the church and if Rita Mendoza would be agreeable to that idea. Tell her we want to make a gift out of the shrimp—you know the rest."

"I'll make some calls?" asked Chelsea.

"I'll be in bed with a box of tissues."

"You don't seem that sad." Chelsea smiled.

I straightened out my bedroom and sat in bed with a bunch of magazines. As I flipped through them I was appalled by an advertisement featuring a blonde sitting on a toilet with her underpants around her ankles; the advertisement was for shoes. I called and canceled my subscription to three magazines that featured the ad. There was something empowering about obliterating the magazines from my life, and I wrote out a check to the National Organization for Women.

By the time I heard my mother and Chelsea talking downstairs, I had cut up a dozen magazines and rearranged all the models so they had three arms and at least two heads.

"Who's still in bed?" asked my mother, climbing the stairs.

I didn't answer. She cautiously opened the door. I saw her stop at the table and inspect the check addressed to NOW.

"This is a strange way for you to celebrate obtaining your own business," she said.

"Well, Jane, I don't really feel like celebrating."

"Why? You managed to procure a very good company."

"And lose my fiancé?"

"I suppose it wouldn't help if I said you can't put a square peg in a round hole." She sat at the edge of the bed and pulled my pinkie toe. My mother took off her jacket and shoes and sat next to me on the bed. "I miss this view," she said.

"You can come and visit anytime you want."

"I heard you have to make an appointment," she laughed.

"What was he like when he got home?" I asked.

"Quiet, very quiet."

"Did you ask what happened?"

"Chelsea had already called in a report. He had a few drinks somewhere else before he came home."

"It was nothing like the fights where we throw things or holler. None of our usual glass breaking."

She put her hand over mine. "I heard there was plenty of broken glass already."

"This week has been a nightmare. I should have known it when Zoe got hitched in Reno. What time is it? I really want a beer."

"Beer and eggs?"

"Yeah, beer and eggs."

I followed my mother into the kitchen. Very little had changed since she lived here. I had new furniture, pots, clocks, and tables, but for the most part things were still located in the same place. She collected random ingredients on the counter. A childhood of poverty makes a creative cook.

"Tell me what is going on," she said, cracking open two beers and handing me one.

"Mom, it is really hard for me to talk about this, knowing how badly you want me to get married."

She let the eggs sit in the bowl and turned slowly to look me in the eyes. Her own eyes were teary and confused. She took one long deep breath and a sip of beer. I felt tightness in my chest.

"If we don't find our own solutions as adults, we try to fix our mistakes through our children." She turned down the flame on the stove. "I want you to get married, or wanted you to get married so I could stop worrying about my mistakes."

Watching my mother cry was immobilizing.

"Your father and I have had some hard times. There are things

I never shared with you. I don't know why. Well, I do know, but I've never been ready to talk about it."

"Jane Lacey, you are surprising me today," I said, swallowing my beer to keep any tears down.

"I'm surprising myself."

She began to work on the eggs. Through her chopping and stirring we continued our conversation.

"Steve and I are finished," I said.

"There is always a moment when we see our partner for who they really are. We choose to love them unconditionally at that time, or we continue to see what we want." She shrugged.

"You never said anything like that before."

"I didn't want you to ask me too many questions," she said, sighing heavily and whipping the eggs.

"Do you think I've always known that I wouldn't marry Steve?"

"We all know things, but we just choose to ignore them until the last possible moment."

I took a long calm breath and a swig of beer. "Like infidelity?"

My mother didn't miss a whip and laid the eggs in the pan. "A perfect example," she said.

She did not turn around or face me. My mother flipped and turned the omelette without breaking her concentration. She kept her back to me. When we were facing one another with our eggs and beer, she sighed. "Infidelity is complicated," she said.

"It seems like marriage is complicated," I said.

"All contracts have fine print."

After thirty years of backbreaking labor and a collection of exquisite shoes, I wondered if my mother was considering leaving my father.

"Mom . . . are you considering a divorce?" I asked.

She looked at me with a tilt of her head and began to laugh. "No, no, honey. It's too late for a divorce, and I hear they're exhausting."

"Then what?"

"Eat your eggs before they get cold."

"I'm not sure you've ever said anything so maternal to me in my whole life."

"I better practice. Looks like you could use a mom right about now."

"Do you remember Johnny McDougal?"

"Of course. He was adorable."

"You remember him?"

"I'd know him anywhere. Those freckles were something to love."

"He doesn't have many left," I said.

"How would you know?"

"I saw him."

My mother dropped her fork.

"What?"

"I saw him on the train the other day when I was stuck. He was sitting right next to me in the dark."

"Is he married?"

"Yes, but not happily."

She patted my hand and smiled. "I'm glad you won't ever have to say that."

All the things I reserved for my conversations with Chelsea I risked saying to my mother that afternoon. We sat in every sunny part of the house, watching the traffic on the pier. By the late afternoon we had split a six-pack and I was ready for a nap.

Chelsea joined us for a glass of wine, and I slept again until the midweek business day was long gone.

There were no lights on in my apartment when I woke. As I lay there I realized that darkness had always come upon our house before someone would turn on the lights. It had become my own habit to wait until the last part of the day was gone before reaching for a lamp. It annoyed Steve whenever he came home to find me sitting in the dark.

I heard soft melancholy voices mixed with sirens. In the darkness of the shadows I saw my mother and Chelsea sitting close to one another on the couch. It was clear that whatever had happened between my father and Chelsea was long enough ago that she and my mother had chosen friendship over resentment.

"Hey, did you drink all the wine?" I asked.

"We thought you might never get up. We have reservations at the River Club in an hour," said my mother in a perky voice.

"The River Club?" I questioned.

"We thought we should celebrate," said Chelsea.

"Celebrate what?"

"Your new business," they said in unison.

"Oh." I wondered if I wanted to get out of my pajamas. I had never really been anywhere with my mother without my father, or out with Chelsea to a place that had tablecloths.

"Chelsea, what happened with the Mendozas?"

"Rocco will transfer the load at the church and give the priest a ride."

"When?"

"Right after the ceremony on Saturday morning."

"Did anyone call Dad and tell him we took care of it?" I asked.

"Call him tomorrow," said my mother. "Get dressed or we'll be late."

During dinner my mother and Chelsea laughed like little girls telling secrets. Though I laughed along with them I felt like an outsider to their long history. It had never occurred to me that in dealing with my father's erratic mood swings and temper they had forged an undeniable bond. We must have gone through four bottles of wine, and I did not remember being dropped off at home, but when the phone rang at three in the morning I was sobered by my father's voice.

"Where is your mother?" he asked.

"Dad?"

"Where is she?"

I looked around the apartment and did not see any traces of her.

"We had a little too much to drink at dinner," I said.

"Where is she?"

"I think she went home with Chelsea."

He coughed.

"Dad, are you OK?"

"Fine. Is Steve gone?" he asked solemnly.

"Not yet." I sat up in bed and realized I still had my shoes on.

"Oh." Silence. "Why didn't you tell me?"

"I don't tell you those things."

"Right."

His response made me feel guilty for sharing my decision with Jane before telling him. In my defense I said: "Sometimes I want to, but you don't seem to want to listen."

"I'm calling you now," he said.

"You're looking for Mom."

"Well, we're on the phone."

I began to strip and realized I was on the phone with my father.

"I arranged for the Mendoza shrimp," I said, changing the subject.

"Thanks."

After some silence I said, "Dad, *I* don't want to marry Steve."

"No one should marry a lawyer," he said.

"I thought you liked him."

"I liked him better than those two-bit hustlers you dated with art projects and finger paints, but that doesn't mean I *liked* Steve."

"Why didn't you ever say anything?"

"You might marry him."

There were new rules for all the old games. I didn't know how to talk to my father or my mother, and now both wanted my full attention.

"Catherine?"

"Yes, Dad. I'm still here."

"At a wedding they say a father's job is to 'Dress up, shut up, show up, and pay up.' Right now I think I should speak up. The truth is I never liked him or his self-satisfied egotistical old man."

For all the times I had ever looked back to see if my parents noticed I was missing, I was suddenly overwhelmed by how closely they had been paying attention. My father, mother, and I were all drunk for the second or third night in a row. It made me wonder what had happened to all of us in the darkness of our houses.

"Dad, I'd like you to come to the office on Friday." I stopped and rephrased the question. "Can you help me in the office on Friday?"

"Sure, sure, I'll be there," he said, and dropped the phone before he hung it up.

7

Refuse Thy Name

There is a fine line between losing and finding yourself again. Thursday morning, as I drank my coffee once again in the living room, avoiding the office, I traced the grout around the new window and began to index my memories of Steve and I together. Putting them into groups proved to me that we had at times been a successful couple.

When I heard Chelsea turn off the office alarm, I pulled a blanket over my head and hid on the couch. Chelsea didn't even bother to check if I was in the office; instead she climbed the stairs. The rituals in my life had disintegrated so quickly.

"Cece?"

"Don't you have a key?" I hollered at the closed door.

Chelsea opened the door and looked around. She did not see me on the living room couch. In the bedroom she picked up my shoes and put them in the closet.

"Where are you?" she asked.

"Living room."

She entered and placed a hand on her hip, a cigarette already smoking between her fingers. "We put you in bed. Are you sleep-walking?"

"I came out here this morning to think."

"Between my hangover and lack of sleep, there is no thinking going on."

"Where's my mother?" I asked.

"She's back up at the house."

"When did she go?"

"This morning. She stayed with me last night," she said. "I'll put on a pot of coffee?"

"My father called. . . ." I stopped myself.

"The old man hates how close your mother and I have become through the years. What did he say?" she asked from the kitchen.

"Oh, nothing. He called about the Mendoza account."

Chelsea hummed and puttered around the kitchen the same way my mother had the day before, and I realized I admired them both for being comfortable with themselves.

"Steve called Basswinder Estate and asked how much money we would lose if there was no wedding."

"Did he call to tell you that?"

"No. They must not have understood where to reach him, because they left the response on my machine," I shouted so she could hear me.

"When did that happen?" she asked, rushing in with a tray of coffee that almost toppled over.

"A day or so ago."

"Why didn't you tell us last night?"

"I didn't want to ruin our celebration."

She kissed me on the forehead and sighed. "Do you have to be so stoic? I wish you weren't like your mother that way. Your father would be screaming, running around, and most likely throwing a few things. In business you're just like him, but in your personal life you just shut down like Jane. Amazing how the genes split."

She returned to the kitchen and came back with a few rolls and butter. "Who put down the money for the deposit?" she asked.

"What?"

"Who paid for the deposit?"

I smiled. "He did."

"Coffee?"

"You know we have tax problems because of the new concession laws. I was holding on to all of my cash capital until the deductibles were posted in January."

"The universe has a plan," she said, and put her feet up on the coffee table. "Maybe *you* don't want to call it off before he does."

"This is not a race." I felt exasperated.

"Have you checked the books?" she asked.

"What books?"

"Etiquette, my dear, etiquette."

"What for?" I asked.

"Maybe the one who ends the engagement has to pay for the losses or something like that."

"I woke up sleeping single in my double bed. That's as far as I got."

"Sounds like a country song." She smiled.

"I think it is."

"You must really be depressed."

"Maybe you can cheer me up by singing 'All My Exes Live in Texas'?"

Chelsea and I were still on the couch trying to figure out who was financially responsible for terminating the engagement when

Emily pushed the doorbell. I had completely forgotten our lunch date. I waited for her at the top of the stairs, in Steve's pajamas for the second day in a row.

"Are you sick?" she asked.

"It depends on how you look at it." I gave her a long hug.

"You smell like cigarettes," she said, walking through the hall.

The apartment was a mess, I was in pajamas, my clothes from the previous night were still on the floor, and the cold coffee sat on the table. Emily looked at me and sighed.

"I haven't seen you leave clothing out since you were almost indicted for laundering money for that Italian family, and I've never seen you in your pajamas past nine a.m. What the hell is going on?"

"We are doing a bit of research," said Chelsea. "Should I order some lunch?"

"Please," I said.

Chelsea stood up and ushered Emily onto the couch. "Your job is to keep her laughing."

"Cigarette?" I asked.

"You don't smoke! What is going on?"

"You look nice and tan. How was Mexico?" I asked.

"We had sex, we had dysentery, and we drank bottled water." She looked down at the large books on the floor. "What exactly are you looking for in the *Modern Book of Events and Etiquette*?"

"The cancellation clause." I tried to smile.

Emily seemed older. As though she'd been married for years, not just moments. We discussed Zoe's elopement only long enough so as not to talk behind her back. Neither of us had heard from her since Sunday, but we had both read the gossip column in the *Daily*.

When I finally told Emily that I was sure Steve and I were ending our engagement she had a few questions: "What did Steve do for you that made you want to spend the rest of your life with him in the first place?"

"I thought he could help me become someone else. You know, that stay-at-home woman with nails and a maid. What about you?"

"Mitchell built a little safety net for all my insecurities."

"You rely on him to support you?"

"Emotionally."

"You were fine before."

"I was always fine, and I'll always be fine, but I feel better with him." She smiled.

Thinking back to the stubborn, argumentative women we were in college lecture halls, it seemed strange to hear her admit she enjoyed his emotional support. "I don't rely on him economically," Emily continued. "That was never our agreement. I wasn't like Zoe in that regard. Sometimes I wish I was."

"You mean seeking the sugar daddy?"

Emily nodded. I thought of my meeting next week where I would see Sid Niceman. I'd broken my rule about dating people in the business for him; I'd been happy with him for months before I realized I was more like a kept woman to him and that he had control over everything we did.

"I could never really marry a sugar daddy," I said.

"I know, but you, me, Zoe—we didn't have the kind of fathers that generously gave their approval. I think it's fine to say we want someone to fill that gap."

"Why do I need to torture myself with pleasing a partner when I can't even please my parents? I thought the last thing I wanted was a guy like my dad—he's such a moody son of a bitch—but at least my father is genuine. Steve is perfect, every woman in the world is crazy for him, but I'm not. Is that OK?"

"If you're comfortable saying it. I look at Mitchell and I'm comfortable. He doesn't have ripples in his stomach and I know that social interaction is a real strain on our friends"—she lifted her eyebrow and lowered her chin for emphasis—"*but,* he gives me something I've been missing since childhood."

"What have you been missing?" I asked.

"That feeling of acceptance. That someone loves me just the way I am." The lids of her eyes were turning pink. "Do you know that at my own wedding my mother was reprimanding me for how the tables were set up? She actually had the nerve to make a snide comment while I was putting on my dress. It started a war. My sisters were going for her throat."

"Was that why you were so late?" I asked.

"We had to wait for everyone to stop crying."

"What about the tiara?"

"Are we allowed to have wine with our lunch?" she asked.

"As many bottles as you want," I said, going to the kitchen and putting two bottles of white wine on ice. I opened up the first one too soon, but we toasted to "nothing."

"OK. Now tell me about the tiara," I pressed.

"My mother inherited it from my grandmother's aunt. It was one of those heirlooms for real Southern belles, not Jewish New Yorkers. My mother thought it was perfect with my dress. You know I searched high and low for that dress. I wanted everything to be simple.

"My mother wouldn't let up about the tiara. Blah, blah about heritage and how difficult it was for the few Jews who had settled in the South. She shoveled on every guilt trip she could conjure. It was like she knew she'd never get another chance to have so much power over me."

"More wine?" I asked, feeling bad that I'd thought the tiara gaudy.

"A lot more." She took a deep breath.

Chelsea came upstairs with two large bags and shook her head. "Emily, it was your job to cheer her up!"

"I did. Doesn't Cece seem very relieved *not* to be getting married?"

After the three of us had lunch I walked Emily downstairs.

"Emily?"

"Yes."

"I don't think I did a good job being a friend during your engagement," I said.

"Why is that?"

"I didn't take the time to *hear* you."

"What do you mean?" she asked.

"I wanted someone different for you. I voiced my opinion to everyone but you. There is not much more we can ask for than that our friends are loved as we love them. Mitchell really does that. I apologize for doubting your decision," I said, looking down at my unpolished nails. They seemed childishly short.

"Sometimes I'm lonely because of my choice. Zoe is going to disappear as a reliable friend. I'm glad to know you want to be there for me."

We held each other for a long time in the doorway. When she turned at the corner and waved, I thought to myself that we become adults in the moment when we can honor each other by telling the truth.

Chelsea met me at the door to our office so I couldn't retreat upstairs so quickly. "Steve called. He wants to see you today."

My body stiffened. "He called to schedule a meeting?" My

feet were cold, and my fingers lost feeling in the tips. "What else did he say?"

"He asked if four-thirty was a good time." Chelsea spoke each word as if she were trying to thread a needle with her lips.

"What time is it now?"

"Two."

"Tell him to be here at four."

"Are you sure?" she asked.

"The longer I wait, the more I'll doubt myself. This is a man I want out of my life as soon as possible."

I went to the roof of our building and walked across the hot sticky tar in my bare feet. I stared up at the Brooklyn Bridge and cursed over the howling trucks and busy streets of the Fulton Fish Market. I yelled into the winds and tried to exhaust my body of anger. If Steve and I were going to meet, I had to get my temper under control so he couldn't use it against me.

I played loud music and straightened out my apartment vigorously, relieving more nervous energy. Whatever happened over the next few hours would lead to an inevitable collapse. I prepared for the storm by battening down my life and throwing away old bottles of sleeping pills and painkillers. The possibility of a drinking bender was strong. Anything that increased the risk of self-destruction needed to be disposed of, and when I finally went down to the office I was calm and focused.

I began researching for next week's meetings. Submerged under a pile of books and notes, I still noticed the rush of traffic and noise when the door opened. Chelsea hit the intercom button.

"Cece?"

"Yes, Chelsea?"

"Steve is here."

"Does he have another lawyer with him?"

"No."

"What is he doing right now?"

"He's looking over the big fish book we use for new clients."

"What did you tell him?"

"I told him you were on the phone to Zanzibar trying to get some Moorish idol fish."

"Chelsea, those are fish for aquariums."

"I was testing him. He failed. Almost two years with you, and he doesn't know an aquarium fish from something you can eat."

"What is he doing now?"

"He is walking toward me because now we're on the phone and he thinks you're done with Zanzibar."

"Tell him I'm on the other line."

I imagine Chelsea held up her hand to stop Steve from coming into my office, but he sailed right by her chartreuse nails and opened the door.

". . . Yes, yes, of course I'll put that order through, and we'll see what I can do about the shipping so their scales don't flake . . ."

With my ear pressed to the phone tightly, I motioned for him to sit.

". . . I understand, let me get back to you with a price if we express it . . . of course. I'll have an answer by five."

"Hello," I said, hanging up the phone.

"Busy day?" he asked without waiting for an answer. "Have you had lunch?"

"Yes."

"I haven't. Should I get something to eat?"

"Do you want to talk?" I asked.

"What about a *late lunch?*" He loosened his tie. "You seem a little edgy—I could skip lunch and take you upstairs?"

The thought of being next to him no longer warmed me. I didn't want anything to do with the memory of our long lunches, afternoon showers, or making coffee in the nude. I had once made a sign that said RESERVED and placed it in the middle of the bed. Steve slipped me a fifty-dollar bill to let him past the door. I never noticed until recently how many games we played to seduce each other; being ourselves was never enough.

"I ate lunch with Emily."

"You look stressed," he said.

"Saffron-blue damsel fish," I said.

"What, are the environmentalists all over you again?"

"No. Saffron-blue damsel fish are tank fish. They are the color of lilacs, except they have an exquisite yellow tail. They can be shipped all over the world and kept in tanks as long as they travel in groups of nine or twelve."

"Find a bigger shipping company," he yawned, and I loathed him for never seeing the tenderness of my world and for never understanding that I loved my fish.

"The male and the female barely tolerate each other. If left alone these fish bicker and destroy each other until they are just shredded scales and fins."

"Is this a puzzle? Speak up, Catherine, because I don't get it."

"We could have never known what was wrong until we got engaged."

"What is wrong now?"

"We were temporary, like a spawning season."

"Can you stop comparing us to fish? Speak logically—I can't understand a word you're saying."

"Logically speaking, you haven't called me in three days," I said.

"I came down here hoping you had cooled off a little. I haven't called you in three days because I wanted you to come to your senses." Steve looked down at his tie and slid the knot up to his neck. "I wanted to walk in here today and be in love with you," he said.

"But you're not. Are you?"

"Are you?"

"Steve, you don't know anything about me. If you did you would know that three days of silence means war, not an apology."

"Sometimes I wonder why you didn't go into the military."

"They didn't accept women for combat until I was past the age."

"You're barely what I consider a woman. You're much closer to being a man. You're on the phone with clients, you're poured over books, and you're even dressed in a suit."

"You want someone to do your laundry and be nice to clients. You want a cupcake, not a woman." After two years together Steve could not see a shred of my insecurity.

"Did you miss me when you lay down to sleep? Do you know I used to fantasize about making love on our honeymoon," he said.

"What happened when we came home?" I asked.

"I don't know."

"The closer you get to that part of the fantasy the less you want me in your life," I said sensibly.

"If you dropped that chip on your shoulder, you could still have me."

"I worked hard for that chip. I've worked every—"

"—every summer day smelling like fish, and grew up with the boys on the docks making fun of you all day long. You never had it easy; you always had it the *hard* way. I know the whole story by heart," he said, leaning on the edge of my desk.

"By the special way you just narrated that life, it seems obvious you don't love that woman; unfortunately *that* is who I am." I took a long, slow, deep breath. "Is there anything else you'd like to say?" I asked.

"Do you want to know why I'm not marrying you?"

"No."

"You should know."

Why did every man convince himself I wanted to hear him even when I said *no*?

"You did this to yourself. I hate the way you try to control our life. Each run we take together I always get the lecture on why I shouldn't sprint at the end. You can't go above Fourteenth Street without making snide comments about anyone with more money than you. Every friend of mine who lives on the Upper East Side is a target for your poverty snobbery. You are so wrapped up in your struggle to control your father's business that you snub every woman who wears lipstick to work and shows off her legs. Not to mention if I leave you alone at a cocktail party, you tell everyone your life story."

I sat motionless, mentally fending off his verbal blows. While sweat ran down my back. His reasons were exaggerations, but just as much was true, and that was the part that hurt. I had presented myself to Steve as the type of women I thought I could be, only to realize I had not been honest with myself—or to him.

"The first time you met my family you blathered on and on about fish. No one cares that much about fish but you and a few Italian jerks who push people around in City Hall."

I barely recognized Steve pacing around my small office.

"Any small request I have, like window-shopping on Madison Avenue, is an attack on your worship of struggle. Your family makes more money off the books in tricky tax deals than I make all year. You can't walk around hating everyone who grew up rich; it's like hating a woman because she's pretty."

"I think you're done," I said.

"I'm not done!"

"I don't want to hear any more," I said as quietly as possible.

"Perfect, you don't even listen to me," he said.

"No, Steve, I hear you now; I also heard you four days ago when you looked into my eyes and told me you loved me."

"I may always love you," he said, "but I don't think I like you." He would not stop. "Are you so proud that you'll let me walk out this door?" he yelled.

"I'm proud, but you have never taken the extra step to meet me halfway. You like to walk out just before I break down. I don't even think you know that I get upset—I cry, too. You're so proud that you walk away before you have to compromise."

"I spend all day in a courtroom compromising."

"Be real! You manage to do all your dirty work behind closed doors. You never compromise in real life, just on paper."

"Should I throw things and break windows?"

"Maybe! Maybe somewhere between broken windows and great exits we could have found a middle ground."

"I've always wanted a smart woman to stand behind me, and I thought you were it," he whined.

"I always wanted someone to stand *beside* me," I yelled.

"Now you want to shove feminist semantics crap at me?"

He did want a woman with opinions, just as long as they all agreed with his. There were women for that. None of them were my friends, but I knew they existed.

"Steve, you will need three women to do what I have done for you. First find a maid to clean up after you, then a personal secretary to follow up on your frequent flier miles, and finally a hooker to be quiet while you curse at her. Now get out of my office," I added as the grand finale.

"If you had gone to some traditional school, instead of those whacked-out expressionist places, you would know . . ." He stopped.

My voice began in a slow tremor and built into a fury: "I would know what?" I asked. "If I went to one of those girls' schools on the Upper East Side, right? Is that what you mean? What would I know if I had been one of them?"

I had begun pounding on the desk with my hand. The message spike that had been a gift from my father, and matched my name plaque, bounced toward me without either of us noticing. When I slammed my hand on the desk the message spike pierced my palm directly under the engagement ring. The resonance of my scream left water rippling in the office's fish tank. Chelsea brought in the first aid kit and withdrew the spike from the webbing between my knuckles. Blood soaked the blotter. She poured me a double Drambuie and wrapped my hand. Steve had gone across the street to get a bucket of ice and never came back.

I threw up twice on my clothes—once from the shock and once from the excruciating pain when I tried to pull off my engagement ring before the entire hand swelled. Chelsea dragged me upstairs to strip my clothes. I convinced her I was fine, and she went to clean up the office before the blood soaked into the carpet. When my parents arrived to take me to the hospital, I was sitting on the kitchen floor in my underwear, sorting through the garbage looking for the painkillers I'd thrown away that afternoon, just hours before.

8

All in the Family

When I opened my eyes, I was in my apartment and the sun was bright behind the drawn shade. I could hear my father talking to Susan. She'd finally arrived from the West Coast, and now she was sitting in my kitchen. A large white gauze mitten on my hand looked like camel toes; my fingers were separated and bound together into two groups. The bandages formed a V that exposed my engagement ring and the yellow-and-purple webbing between my fingers. The ice pack that had melted on my bed felt like a warm jellyfish against my thigh. I could tell my mother had slept next to me because the sheets smelled like lilac soap.

Susan's voice had the same fluctuations since puberty. If I didn't know we were close to thirty I would say she was still a teenager. She spoke with a funny mixture of pubescent slang and a Spanish gang vocabulary that came from teaching seventh grade in the California ghettos. My father was probably very confused, but he would never interrupt her to ask exactly what *vato* or *homey* actually meant.

"Yeah, I take care of my little *vatos*. They are strictly home-boys with hair nets on the street, but in my classroom . . ."

My mind filled with lists and things I should do. I was thinking about the tie Steve had at my dry cleaners when Susan checked on me.

"Awake?"

"Unfortunately."

She knelt beside me and wrapped her arms around my shoulders. I held on to her with my good hand and gauze mitten. She whispered into my ear that I was an incredible woman, listed my accomplishments, special qualities, and told me she loved me just the way I was. My hand throbbed. I was hungry, sick, scared, and relieved.

"I think it's really OK," I said.

"He was a jerk," she said.

"What did my father tell you?"

She rolled her eyes. "I don't think he understands me. Actually your mother and Chelsea told us the whole story, or *her* version of the story. Is that what you wanted to talk about before I left California to come East?"

"I guess, but I didn't really know then."

"Why didn't you call me in Pennsylvania? I was so bored down there. Everyone is running around like chickens all stressed out, and they keep telling me to relax."

"Do you fit into the dress?" I asked.

Susan's family had passed down the same wedding dress since the early 1900s. The dress had exquisite craftsmanship with one hundred silk-covered buttons down the back. It was originally made for her great-grandmother, a petite, thin woman. Susan was small, but she liked tortilla chips, salsa, and a few beers with her dinner.

"Weight Watchers fit me into that tradition; now let's hope I can keep it off."

"Only one week to go."

"Easy for you, marathon girl. We've been collecting masses of food at our house for guests and the rehearsal dinner barbecue."

"Speaking of barbecue, I might not feel up to the engagement party this weekend."

"I understand—I'm sure Jeannine and Enrique will, too. Your parents want to bring you out to their house anyway."

I pulled a pillow over my head.

"*Why* didn't you call me?" she asked.

"I don't know. I just wanted to see what happened."

"Who really dumped who?" she asked.

"It was mutual. I'm confused about who should take care of all the financial aspects of the cancellation. I would feel bad for his secretary, because he'll make her do all the work, but she'll probably wind up with this engagement ring." I held up my hand.

"If you ever get it off," she laughed.

"I wish they had cut it off. I can't remember anything from yesterday. I started drinking from the bottle the moment the spike went through my palm."

"What did he say that made you so angry? Chelsea said you were slamming your desk and screaming at him to get out."

"What *his* reasons were for calling it off?"

"Well? What were they?"

"The chip on my shoulder."

"What?"

"The list; the way I make fun of people who live on the Upper East Side, I lecture him about sprinting at the end of his run, he doesn't like that I talk openly at cocktail parties, and he thinks

I'm boring because I talk too much about fish. He hit all the sore spots."

"For real? He said those things?"

"For real."

"What did he do when you hurt yourself?"

"He told Chelsea he was getting ice, and then he split," I sighed.

"I thought at least one of us should marry a rich guy so we could have some fun, but he was a complete joke! Are you going to keep the ring?"

"What would I do with it? It has a curse."

"I bet it would fit me." She smiled.

"Should I give it to you as a wedding present?"

"It might buy me a new truck to cruise around my California suburb."

"I don't think so," I said, trying to sit up.

She looked at me quizzically. "Were you so drugged out you don't know why they didn't cut it off last night?"

"What are you talking about?"

"Your mother told me they wanted to cut it at the hospital, but they didn't want the responsibility to pay for it if something went wrong. It's worth twenty-seven thousand dollars."

I looked at the sharp clarity of the ring and felt my stomach turn. *What?*

"Steve's mother mentioned the price of the ring at the wedding shower. When you were freaking out and washing all those dishes his mom said something like 'Cece should be a little more careful with a twenty-seven-thousand-dollar ring on.' Your mother was appalled."

I thought about how often I had left the ring in my gym bag or on the side of the sink. Like most engaged women, in the beginning I compared it to other rings, adoring the clarity, setting, and crisp appearance. My ring was big, but I had never really taken the "rock" jokes to heart. Enamored by the fact that I had a ring, I stared at it for the first few months, but eventually I grew accustomed to having it on my hand.

Susan took my good hand. "Too much right now? Huh?"

"Maybe," I said.

"Do you want some coffee?"

"And a glass of water?"

"Sure." She stood.

"Hey? Where is your teaching friend Tanya?"

"Your mom is showing her around the seaport and picking up some things for lunch. We'll head up to Times Square later and walk through the park."

"I'm sorry I can't show you around."

"Your mother is doing a great job. Besides, Tanya said your situation could be worse."

"How?"

"At least you didn't find out after the wedding it was a mistake. She has two kids and an ex-husband who lags on child support and alimony."

"True, I only get stuck with a dress."

"And maybe a ring. If you want to get rid of the dress, you can always put an ad in the paper. Wanted: Single White Female for wedding. No expenses, no guarantees. Fresh oyster bar. Contact fraternity jerk at Scudder, Scudder, Skipowitz and *whatever,* by September fifth."

"The scary part is that some women would call," I said.

"With his secretary? He'd never get the messages." She winked and shut the bedroom door behind her.

*   *   *

My mother collected the wedding file, some books, and notes on my desk and packed them in a small bag. I recorded a message on my machine that anyone looking for me could call my parents' house and anyone calling for Steve should call his apartment. It gave me a little thrill to leave his unlisted number. I planned to spend the next few days taking painkillers and drinking by the pool. I would see the doctor again on Monday to test for any permanent damage to my tendons and nerves.

To be in the backseat of a car with my parents filled me with a defeated sense about life. After throwing up on the parkway, I moved next to my father in the front. He watched my mother in the rearview mirror so intently he barely noticed when I threw up again out the window. No one but Susan had dared to ask exactly what was finally ending our engagement. Since I assume Chelsea's ear had been glued to the wall, they knew everything anyway.

I already had messages when we arrived home. I dropped my sweater on the floor like a teenager and sat outside on the deck to watch the sunset.

It made me feel safe to be at my parents' house, to listen to the lapping sound of the Hudson. My parents lived in a traditional widow's house. A few decades ago my mother would have waited for my father to come home from sea, watching out the huge bay window for his ship. I wondered if they watched the water questioning who would be alone first.

If I had grown up in this house I would have been a spoiled child with thick metal watches and dirty pearls. Instead my goals were centered on money, as if being successful in business could ease the feelings I had as a child. Sometimes I bordered on nasty; my opinions flowed like a loudmouth bigot in a bar. Ironically men adored being around me when we were in groups; I was always more interesting than the well-groomed girls at uptown parties. However, when alone with one man he quickly tired of my dominating nature. I gave Steve a tremendous amount of credit for holding out the longest.

I didn't ask for a drink, but my father brought me one of his special old-fashioneds. He carried the portable phone in his pocket.

"You'll need this," he said, and put the phone on the table between us. "How's the hand?"

"It's just a paper cut," I said.

"Sometimes I wish you were a boy." He brushed his white dry hair out of his eyes and then rubbed his palms back and forth over his knees. "I don't know what to say."

"If I was a boy, would you know what to say?" I asked.

"If you were a boy you wouldn't expect me to *say* anything. We could just sit here in silence and that might be enough."

"Why don't you think that is enough for me?"

"Who raised you to be so tough?" he asked.

"You want to talk?" I asked.

"We talked when I called the other night," he said.

"You were drunk."

"Let's just watch the sun go down. Over the weekend I want you to know about a new project I'm working on. It's on our agenda for Monday, and I need you to be ready." He took a long sip of his drink.

"I've already started on the notes for Sid Niceman and his crew," I said.

"This is something else you might have more fun with."

"What is it?" I asked.

He smiled. "I thought you didn't want to talk."

"I don't want to talk about my ex-fiancé, my overpriced wedding dress, my honeymoon, or my inability to have a relationship. I can always talk about business."

"Did I do that to you?"

"No, Dad, and yes. I'm not a woman for every man, but I can't keep blaming you and Mom. You taught me everything you knew about life and everything you knew about fish. Mom taught me whatever she knew about being a woman, which wasn't as much as I might have liked, but she did make sure I knew how to be independent. It doesn't make anyone responsible for my mistakes."

"Why did you love him, Cece?"

"Because he wasn't at all like you," I laughed.

"I'm confused then. Why didn't you work at it?"

I patted him lightly on the knee and said: "Because he wasn't enough like you."

If there were a moment when I realized my parents were growing older, it was in my father's responses. Sentimentality comes with age, and when I watched the edge of his dirty gray eyes water, I accepted his proximity to heaven. I was glad I hadn't missed the opportunity to tell him I loved him in my own way.

My mother came out to join us. She slipped a plastic bag around my wounded hand and told my father to keep it submerged in the ice bucket she placed between us. She pulled up a chair and sat on my right side. The smoke from their cigarettes kept the mosquitoes away. Once the sun was gone, the house grew dark. We sucked on oranges coated in sugar from our drinks and listened to the phone ring.

I returned some phone calls on Saturday and quietly announced my canceled engagement to my closest friends. The injury to my hand was the comic twist I used at the end of my story to give the whole argument a slapstick quality. It helped people believe I would survive. My mother made all my favorite fish dishes, and I ate all day long and stayed up late watching television, eating ice cream covered in crème de menthe.

Sunday was a slow, groggy morning filled with reading the paper and discussing the details of canceling the wedding. My mother began to keep a list of topics that needed to be addressed. I admired her perfect script, all traces of individuality cast out from the snap of a nun's ruler across her knuckles. She wrote: *dress, shoes, wedding hall, invitations, bridesmaid gowns, flowers, shower gifts, registry, monogrammed items*—and finally, underlined three times, was *engagement ring*. After the breakfast dishes were cleared they both sat across from me.

My mother asked: "Will you change your mind even if he does?"

"It's too late," I said.

My mother sighed and my father nodded. They both bobbed their heads for a moment, digesting my sentiments and the entire situation. Before asking any more questions, my father closed his eyes, sat back in his chair, and crossed his arms over his stomach. My mother stood and kissed his forehead. She whispered something soothing in his ear that I did not hear and rested her hands on his shoulders; then she glanced over at me with a closed-lip smile. The table was covered in local Sunday papers and the *New York Times*. My father sat forward and slid his hand under the weekly magazine. When he pushed away the glossy magazine I saw grainy black-and-white photograph reproductions under his palm and fingers. The back page of the *Sunday Times* lists items of social interest; it was a sign of your stature and cultural interest if your engagement or wedding was noted. Throughout college it was the one thing a gaggle of girls would reach for in the dining hall; it is the sports page for single women.

My father stared down at the page.

My mother patted his shoulder. "Go on," she said.

When I look back, it was probably an odd moment for William and Jane Lacey. Their only daughter, heir to the family business, sat medicated, hungover, and wounded in their first formal dining room with matching silverware. On her finger was an engagement ring worthy of her affection but swollen to her hand like a scarlet letter. The Laceys were no longer part of the downtrodden working class with no future; they had a two-car garage on a nice waterfront piece of land, even if it was just up the river. Catherine Lacey was walking away from a union that would continue to elevate them. What I loved about my parents right then was I knew they didn't give a damn.

As my father slid the paper toward me I needed only a glimpse of the photograph to know that Steve and I had made it to the back-page announcements. In the photograph Steve and I had generous smiles, pearly teeth, chunky watches, and all the correct clothing for a couple ready to merge their incomes. I thought of Steve's proposal in the paper, and I laid my head down on the table and began to cry. My parents rose and came to my side. Their arms were wrapped so tightly around me that I felt their fingers on my ribs as I gasped for air between sobs.

My mother wiped the newsprint off my forehead and gave me two bags of ice: one for my eyes and one for my hand. The first phone call we answered was from Steve's mother, Gail. It was agreed that our parents should mediate to accomplish things as soon as possible.

The invitations had been completed by the calligrapher, and

Steve's family would use the preaddressed envelopes to send out personalized cancellation notices. Basswinder was apologetic they could not return the deposit but wondered if I could send a sample of tuna and rates for upcoming menu requests. The bridal shower gifts were still in Steve's parents' garage; once I forwarded the addresses Gail would return them appropriately (no doubt with a little note of her own). A small argument arose over who should reimburse people for monogrammed items. My mother insisted that due to the expense of the dress and bridesmaid gowns it was not our responsibility to worry about monogrammed gifts. The bridal shop would accept bridesmaid dresses back if none of them had been altered. My dress would be cleaned and professionally sealed after I came in for a final fitting. *My* frequent flier miles had bought our honeymoon airline tickets, and Steve's firm had received several free rooms to stay at one of the large Caribbean resorts. If I changed all the reservations for our honeymoon from the third week of September to the last days of August I could take my vacation directly after Susan's wedding. There was no problem switching dates at the resort since I was exchanging the beginning of peak season for the less desirable hurricane weather.

Steve's mother called several more times and eventually gave my mother a bank branch, in Manhattan, where they had a safety deposit box. His mother requested that I drop the ring off as soon as possible, to which my mother said: "As soon as Steve comes back with the ice," and hung up.

Our families had dissolved the plans that had been the backbone of our arguments with irritating dexterity. I was relieved; it seemed easier to face my colleagues and friends with the disintegration of my engagement than to ask myself why I was walking down the aisle in a dress. I was not the woman who had wanted expensive calligraphy or rose-scented invitations. It wasn't my idea to register for china or sit down to a five-course meal. All-night dancing on the docks, a buffet, an open bar, a seafood grill and ice-cold beer would have suited me better than sorbet after each course. Everyone accepted the end of our courtship. Losing their privilege of being bridesmaids did not upset my friends; they only wanted to be assured that I would not go back to him. My father and I would have a tough week catching each other up on everything around the office, but I felt it was better to go on vacation and break the spell of memories around my apartment.

Without a change of scenery I might stay home lamenting. A clean break was reward enough, and the excitement of a vacation would help me get through Susan's wedding. By next Sunday, as the party broke up, I would fly off to the Caribbean and catch my breath. Steve would have to answer any remaining questions and details.

I knew him well enough to believe he would have doubts. Alone in his apartment, with newspapers, take-out food containers, and dirty dress socks, he would convince himself he had made a mistake. Knowing no one was waiting for him after work would increase his desperation. He would persuade himself he missed me, but it would only be that he missed having *someone.*

9

An Honest Day's Work

My parents forbade me to take the train back to New York alone on Sunday night. I agreed to stay since my father would be driving in Monday morning for the meeting we scheduled last week but had never had. Of course, that meant we would be on fishmonger time. At four in the morning my mother came into my room with coffee.

"Are you for real?" I asked.

"Your father is excited to be with you."

"I'm exhausted."

"He wants to get a full day in, before you have to go to the doctor."

"I don't think there's any permanent damage," I said, wiggling a few fingers.

The fine wrinkles around her mouth and eyes disappeared in the blue predawn light. "Are you sure you can do this?"

"What?"

"Stop being so tough for me, OK? I know you've got balls made of steel. You inherited them from me. However, you also have my inability to let anyone know when you're experiencing pain."

"What choice do I have, then, but to keep going?"

She handed me the coffee and sat down on the bed. "Enjoy having your father by your side; he's so lonely for your friendship." She paused.

"Thanks, Mom." I took her hand in the dark, pulled her closer to me, and then rested my head on her shoulder.

"Come home whenever you want—you're always welcome."

"Is something wrong?" I asked.

"Promise you won't try and solve everything by yourself."

"I'll try not to."

"Do you want to wear my blue-striped suit down to the city today?" she asked.

"Are you trying to tell me I won't have time to run upstairs and change once Dad gets me into the office?"

"He has big plans for you."

When she kissed my forehead I felt safe.

There was no traffic at five in the morning, but my father rushed us like we were late. Growing up with fishermen means that at dawn your day is half over. William Lacey was always at his best in the morning; perhaps every Irishman is. By four o'clock in the afternoon most of them are too drunk or too tired for conversation. His freckled hands controlled the wheel like a tugboat captain. He made very slight movements to adjust the steering and relied on instinct to guide him around potholes.

"The Mendozas called to say everything was excellent, but Dominic wondered why Father Labrea had to pick up the shrimp from the church."

"Tax-deductible donation to a charitable cause," I said. "Rocco dropped it off with Father Labrea so I could write it off."

"You didn't send the Mendozas a *bill?*"

"I thought it was a gift," I said defensively.

"It wasn't."

"Everything the Mendozas have ordered for the past twelve years has been a gift, why shouldn't the shrimp be?" I asked.

"They know that kind of butterfly shrimp is expensive."

"Whatever." It looked like a long week ahead.

"Whatever," he said playfully.

This was not my father. Recent events were taking a larger toll on my parents than expected; I was left to wrestle with all forms of their unpredictable behavior. I ignored him for as long as I could. There were a few items I had in my apartment from the wedding shower that would have to be sent to Steve's mother. A thin veil of dust had settled on the Strausberg Flowers pitcher and cake plate, the brass alarm clock, the sterling silver picture frame with green enamel, the Waterford crystal tumblers, and the Swiss Army Champ knife in eighteen-karat gold with twenty-nine functions.

"Are you listening to me?"

"No." I shrugged, because I wasn't.

"Does the hand hurt?"

"No." I shrugged, because it didn't.

"Should I keep talking about the consulting project?" he asked.

"I was thinking about the first time I gutted a fish," I said.

"You did that before they cut your umbilical cord."

Hooked through the mouth with their gills spread open like a blooming rose, the fish dangled from my father's hand. An open sliver from the kitchen curtain allowed the sun to glisten on their scales. The smell of salt water blew through the house. My father hurled the fish onto a spread of newspaper and argued with my mother; she didn't like to clean and gut. On the edge of the kitchen door between the pantry and bathroom, perhaps just four years old, I stood sucking on my finger, curious and interested. He waved for me to come closer. While my parents bickered over whether I might have nightmares after cutting open the flesh, it was too late; I had already begun to pop out the eyes of each fish with a butter knife.

"Are you still as good at cleaning?" My father patted me on the knee and smiled.

"Almost. I haven't practiced. It is not a talent most men appreciate," I said.

"Maybe you haven't found the right man."

"Maybe," I said.

A wet heavy sigh slipped through my father's nose.

"Am *I* consulting for Sid Niceman on the new restaurant uptown?" I asked.

"You are."

"So whom are you consulting for?"

"Anne Tulley at *The Explorer.*"

"That fancy travel magazine?"

"You know it?"

"Steve always ordered it for his waiting room."

"Figures."

"How did you meet her?" I asked.

"At the Classic Ships Convention Dinner."

"Where was Mom?"

"Please, you know your mother hates—"

"—Dinner for more than two," I finished the sentence.

"The magazine is looking for some high-end culturally stimulating adventures. Anne wants—"

"Oh, we call her Anne already?"

"My charm is all I got left now that you run things downtown. I told you last week we needed a meeting about this."

A small tense chill knotted itself in the center of my back. After taking a deep breath I waved him along as if I were casually directing him toward a parking spot. "Please, continue."

"Anne was looking for some classy ships to do one of her fashion layouts with some deep-sea fishing."

"And you convinced her it would be more fun to see a bunch of cute guys get seasick on salt-worn, patched up, ragged little dink boats?"

"Couldn't have said it better."

"What do we have to do? Set them up with some guys down in the Keys or with some Micronesian-island spear fishermen who stand on poles?"

"I'll take care of that. Your job is to choose the models and photographers."

"Why?"

"You can choose some boys tough enough to hang out with Charlie Andrews on the *St. Thomas Spirit* or the whole thing goes flat. You're the one who knows the crew of fishermen in most of the countries we deal with. You're the trained dockhand."

"What an art form," I sighed.

"I told Anne that you travel, you're the family athlete, and you're the one to decide which guys can handle the anchors."

"Just because I like to run marathons in old European cities and go fishing in Hong Kong doesn't mean I'm an expert traveler or I'm qualified to pick models."

"You don't see *me* windsurfing in Spain or mountain biking through the Austrian and Swiss border. You travel, you do sports, and you'll know who the right men are for the job."

"If you sold this whole pitch on the fact that there needs to be chemistry between the crew and the people on the fashion shoot, you are insane! Charlie Andrews doesn't even have a personality until his sixth beer."

"I sold the idea based on the ecotour reality trend. This world is too smart for fakes anymore. People who made fast money want to know what authentic work is like. Anne Tulley purchased the chance to send some boys down to Ole Andrews and see what they catch *for real*."

"And you convinced her that calluses, bloody fingers, torn off nail beds, seven-day beard growth, and dark rum hangovers are going to make for better pictures?"

"Yes. Some ignorant crew of city dwellers isn't going to piss off our one-in-a-million fisherman in the Dominican Republic! I want to make sure we pick at least decent jerks to travel the waters."

"I can't do it, Dad. It's out of my realm."

"You can."

"What if I don't want the job?"

He smirked. "Have some fun with the models."

"Dad," I sighed.

"Now just listen, a little distraction might be a good thing."

"This is way out of my league."

"We don't have the final say on who travels in the end anyway."

"I won't do it."

"You form an opinion about people in two minutes or less. I've never known you to hold back. I'm giving you the opportunity to be paid for being critical."

"You're trying to set me up."

"I'm trying to expand your client base."

"I like fish; I want to deal with fish. You can deal with this little sham."

"It's a shamrock," he said, and exaggerated one of his silly flirtatious winks. "What are you afraid of, Cece?"

It had not occurred to me that I was scared until then. Slowly I was convincing myself that I was a failure—and my father knew it, too. He knew that I judged myself harshly and that feeling I had erred was enough to cost me a chunk of my self-esteem. Since there were no marathons I could run to regain what I was losing, I turned my attention back to work.

Complete exhaustion had set in by nine o'clock in the morning. The phone started ringing before office hours, and the ink ran out on the printer. I had fallen asleep at my desk when I heard the intercom buzz.

"Telephone call."

"Who?" I barked.

"You are hungry, grumpy, and suffering from a caffeine crash, *and* you have a phone call from a haughty-sounding British woman, a Ms. Tulley, at *The Explorer.*"

"Ugh. What else can happen in this day?"

"God always has a plan," she said.

"Hello, Ms. Tulley," I said as calmly as possible.

"Please do call me Anne." I bet she spelled that *A-n-n-e.* "How is it all progressing?"

"Who could really complain about a dozen men who look like models about to knock on your door?"

"Too bad they really are models," she laughed. "Your father was so worried about the dynamics of the trip. I tried to tell him that most of the models don't even have personalities. There is rarely a need to trifle over group *dynamics*. But isn't it fun, anyway?"

"I suppose—we haven't really begun."

Instead of playing the corporate lion-and-mouse game, where one remains quiet and the other is forced to speak out of nervousness, I decided to be the lion and open my big fat mouth.

"The concept is three men in a boat, right?" I asked again, wondering if my father had it correct.

"Conceptually speaking, my dear, it is 'Three wise men from Gotham, who went to sea in a bowl. If the bowl had been stronger'—well, you know . . ." Her voice turned frigid. The use of an authoritative tone was necessary or she would take over the conversation and disregard my opinions. Women's rules for power are tougher to understand than men's.

"Mother Goose, of course."

"Weren't you a fan?"

"Never, but I always like going out to sea."

"That's why we hired you. Pick the prissy pretty ones who can take it. I might even start hauling some things around after your father told me that loading down on the docks is the best upper-body workout a girl can get."

Just then Chelsea held her finger down on the intercom to make a long obnoxious sound and interrupt my conversation. "The first model has arrived," she announced.

"Already? Where's my father?"

"He stepped out," she said with annoyance.

"Manipulative old curmudgeon. Can you make a new pot of coffee?" I pleaded.

"Of course. Here comes the first one."

"Anne?"

"Yes, well, now comes the fun. Call me in a few hours."

The model was six feet three with brown hair that stopped at his jawbone. His laugh lines gave him an educated appearance.

"So you're the fish lady?"

I nodded.

"I've done quite a bit of fishing," he said.

"That must have been rewarding. May I see your portfolio?" I asked, not knowing what else to do or say.

I flipped through the pages of the pictures without paying attention.

"I thought this was more of a 'get to know you' type of thing. The agency said it would be about chemistry." He smiled.

"What are you talking about?"

He scanned over the paintings on the far wall, avoiding further eye contact.

"Do you have any questions?" he asked.

I glanced down at his headshot. "Do you, Mr. Rite?"

"Call me Alexander. Do I have questions about the trip or about you?" He crossed his legs, assuming a more comfortable position. I shut his portfolio and handed it back to him.

"Is my interview over?"

"I have lots of young men to interrogate." I extended my good hand to say good-bye.

He stood at the door, lingering. "You're funny—I like you. I'm having dinner tonight with a few friends—would you like to join us?"

"I'm not good in groups."

"If you change your mind, we'll be at Chow Chow." He smiled as if everyone eventually changed plans for him.

I didn't look up again until I heard the door shut.

"Chelsea? How many more are out there?" I asked, feeling a growing anger at my father.

"Six. Three from someplace called Boss, one from Ford, and two from, hum . . . can't pronounce it."

"Are any of them really worth looking at?"

"They are all worth *looking* at."

By the time I'd seen eight men, two seemed appropriately suited to handle the trip if they could get their mothers to pack for them. They had exotic names, long hair, and wardrobes that consisted of leather jackets and white T-shirts.

"I'm ready for the next one."

"Sean from Ford on the way in."

His good looks already seemed standard: blond, young kid, backpack, white T-shirt, and in-line skates. I would even bet he waxed his eyebrows. He said nothing and stared at the floor. I was distracted by how concentrated he was at not making eye contact. Not that I was an expert, but his photographs were very good—a lot of outdoor exposure.

"Have you ever really fished before?" I asked.

"I'm a boy. I've put live worms on a hook and stuck them in the water."

This was the type of smug little egoist I'd like to reject. "Yeah? I've seen pretty boys put on hooks and stuck in the water with cement shoes, too."

After a long silence he said, "Are you any good at fishing?"

"I've forgotten how to be patient." I paused. "What I really know is shipping and handling, but I'm still pretty impressive at gutting."

He pointed to my hand. "Is that how you injured yourself?"

"No." I shook my head. "I'm not very gracious today. Do you need some coffee or to use the bathroom?"

"No, thanks. I feel bad about how I reacted to your first question. Would you be embarrassed if I apologized?" He tugged at a few of his leg hairs so the skin stood away from his thigh.

"Do you really need to?"

"I reacted badly in the beginning of our interview."

"Fine," I said with a genuine smile.

"The rumor out in the waiting room is that you're a real nightmare, but I think you're not really ripping people apart, you just want to get beyond their surface."

My face flushed. "I'm trying to do something I'm underqualified for, and my only chance at looking professional is being a bitch. Now you know my secret—what's yours? Why are you modeling?"

"I'm trying to make money for school."

"What do you study?" I asked.

"Oceanography. I was an intern for a marine life-recycling project. Some famous designer wanted me to model in his fashion show, and before I knew what happened I wound up here. A fish out of water, so to speak. The benefit is that I am closer to my mother. You kind of remind me of her."

The expression on my face must have been shocked and appalled.

"Don't misunderstand," he said. "You have the same sense of humor."

"Where does she live?" I asked.

He smiled. "Allenwood Penitentiary."

"I like her already."

*   *   *

When the last model left I did not hesitate to call Anne back to share my insights.

"Hello, Anne—Cece Lacey."

"You are fast!"

"There isn't that much to go on."

Anne laughed heartily. "Told you, darling. Wait, at least the photographers are more interesting."

"I've selected three men. Two are in the younger category and similar to fraternity boys spending Dad's money."

"Talk to me about the fraternity boys."

"Sean, a blonde, from Ford."

"Good reputation. No drug offenses, and I am sure he's never stayed out late drinking. I think he even has a sick mom somewhere that he sends a monthly check to."

"For the crazy redhead freckle thing—"

"—Kyle from Boss?"

"Yes. Any past misdemeanors?" I asked.

"No. Two good kids. Continue."

"For the moody pensive type I thought of Alexander Rite or Randy Trip."

"Alexander Rite? Tall thin guy with glasses?"

"That's him." I was impressed with her knowledge of all the models. At the time it did not occur to me that she had slept with most of them.

"A bit old for the other two, unless we do the older brother thing. He makes a great first impression, but works too many angles all at once. You can't be there for the cameras and screw the client."

"What about Randy?" I ask, feeling my credibility slip.

"Randy? Brownish-honey hair?"

"Green eyes." The intercom light illuminates without sound. "Can you hold?" I ask.

"Fine."

"What, Chelsea? I'm trying to nail down some details."

"Don't be a tyrant. Some model named Alexander is on the line—he stressed it was urgent."

"Put him on hold."

"Anne? Anne? Shit! Chelsea! Will you get Anne Tulley from *The Explorer* on the line?"

"I'm still here," she sighed. She spoke in a flippant tone. "I won't tie you up. I like your choices."

"Anne, please, Hong Kong can wait. It's only shipping."

Always accentuate someone's importance, I thought as Anne continued: "Good combinations. Boys from the crowded city of Gotham out with a first-year salary bonus from some financial firm and then rigged into hard labor. I see them ready to blow away the blues with a fishing trip and wind up in the real world. Are we starting in the Atlantic or Pacific?"

"It depends on the dates you select."

I heard Anne take another long drag of her cigarette. I envisioned what kind of woman she was: early forties, a husband and maybe a lover, male or female. She wore dark wine-colored lip liner because it looked good on the edge of her martini glass, and she hadn't worn a pair of low-heeled shoes since fitted skirts were invented. She was a woman I admired but could never emulate.

"There are really only a few good photographers to choose from. Call me when you've looked though their portfolios. However tempting, refrain from dating the models you're considering for the trip. Oh, wait—you're getting married, aren't you?"

"Actually, no. I'm not."

"But I just saw it yesterday in the *Times*," she said.

"Ironic, isn't it?"

"Should I extend condolences to you?" she asked.

"To him, of course!" I said with as much empty enthusiasm as possible.

She laughed. "I've had three mediocre marriages, an annulment, and two great divorces! Have some fun with the models before they know you haven't selected them."

"Have you spoken with my father about this?"

"He's such a charm. What a spunky little Irishman." Anne spoke like a woman who knew her game well. "Don't take anyone seriously but *me*. Remember I have the real say on everything and everyone who travels. We'll have coffee soon to do some itinerary planning. *Ciao,* for now."

"Ciao."

The hold button kept the first model I saw waiting. The red pulsing light was like a candy I shouldn't taste.

"Hello—remember me?"

"Alexander Rite, older, hair to his jawbone. I have plans."

"Want to hear your horoscope?" he asked.

"I'm an Aries. What does *Vanity Fair* have to say for this month?"

"How did you know it was *Vanity Fair* magazine?" he asked.

"Is there another bible for the well-dressed but not yet famous?"

"Well, Aries, it sounds like time to throw out old luggage, including people that you've stood by too long. Have some fun and get with a program that beckons you to ignite it with your Ram torch."

"Did you make that up?"

"I'm not even paraphrasing."

"And your horoscope?" I ask.

"I should clean up my act and deal with a conglomerate of paperwork."

"Accurate?"

"I haven't paid my taxes."

"It's August!"

"I know, I know. I was distracted by other things."

Poor people always know how much their bills are because they can't afford to pay them; wealthy people need their bills to remind them of how much they spend.

"So what about dinner?" he asked.

"Plans."

"We'll be going to a club after. I'll leave your name at the door."

Chelsea waved lunch in front of me.

"I have to go."

"I'll see you later."

"Maybe." Maybe?

I sat at my desk and inspected the bruise around my finger. It was a growing fungus with ripples of dark veins and a greasy veneer from the doctor's ointment. The clear glassy diamond looked like the watchful eye of an alligator breaking the surface.

The phone rang and I answered before Chelsea, expecting it to be the model, *"Maybe."*

"I had you in my book for tonight," answered Zoe defensively.

"Zoe?"

"Yes."

"Are we supposed to meet tonight?" I asked.

"Yes, did you forget?"

"Completely. I've been a little crazy."

"Who did you think I was?"

"Steve," I lied.

"Not getting along?" she asked.

"Not getting married."

"I just saw your announcement in the *Times!*"

"We'll talk about it tonight."

"Where should we have dinner?"

"You choose—I can't really think right now," which was not a lie.

"Just come to my apartment around seven."

"How's married life?" I asked.

"It already feels like an eternity."

There is a freedom in being your own boss that balances the albatross of working for yourself. I noticed though that I had begun to take extensive liberties with my time and the grunt work was piling itself up on Chelsea's desk. Still, I needed to take time for myself. I decided to call Emily for advice.

"I'm going to see Zoe for dinner. Can you think of any good things I can say about Aaron?"

"He owns a bar and has an interest in keeping it open."

"To support his alcoholism," I replied.

"Better than Zoe supporting him."

"Remember that guy from the woods of Vermont?" I asked.

"He wasn't all that bad, I liked him."

"He was convicted of carrying a loaded shotgun in the state of New York."

"Can't we assume that was a cultural difference?" she laughed.

"Driving with a loaded shotgun in Vermont is socially acceptable but still illegal," I said.

"I have to go into a meeting. Can I call you later? Oh—how's the hand?" she asked sweetly.

"Ugly."

"Did you tell Zoe about Steve?"

"Briefly."

"Talk about yourself and stay clear of Aaron."

"Do you think I need therapy?" I asked.

"That's a longer discussion. Can you come out to our beach house this weekend?"

"Susan's wedding is on Saturday."

"Your friend from the West Coast? The one you met at the United Nations camp?"

"Right."

"Let's talk before you leave for your—"

"Honeymoon."

"Vacation."

"Can't I just leave you suicidal messages when I'm alone in the hotel?"

"Not funny," she said in a warning tone.

"Bye."

By the time I returned to the office, after my doctor's appointment, my father and Chelsea were no longer there, but each had left me a long detailed list of things that occurred. Attached to the list were two pieces of scrap paper in my father's handwriting. One said I should call my mother and report what happened at the doctor's office. The other was an address, the address of the club where the model would be this evening. My father must have enjoyed taking that message tremendously. I went upstairs and began collecting a few of Steve's things in a box. The phone rang seven times on the office line and then immediately on my private number.

"Why haven't you called?" asked my mother.

"I'm exhausted and I wanted to pack a few of Steven's things before my dinner with Zoe tonight."

"Did you have a good day?"

"I suppose. It is a very good time in my life to terrorize attractive men."

"What did the doctor say about the hand?" she asked.

"There is feeling in the tips of all my fingers and wrist. The X ray showed nothing spliced or broken. He said I was very lucky and pierced the skin and webbing below the knuckles. He cleaned the hand and rewrapped it, but I couldn't watch because it made me sick." I stacked the gift boxes from Tiffany & Co. in three large shopping bags while we talked.

"What will you do for Susan's wedding?"

"I'm having the bandage changed on Thursday, before I head down to Pennsylvania. He said he could cover the white gauze."

Before she had time to ask another question the buzzer rang.

"Hold on, Mom, someone is at the door."

When I looked out the window, no one was there. I pressed the intercom to ask who it was and heard keys jingling in the lock.

"I think Chelsea forgot something."

"Chelsea's having dinner with us tonight; she's getting out of the car with your father right now. Who's at the door?" she asked. There was only one other person who had keys.

"He's there, isn't he?" she asked.

"I think so."

"Who else has keys?"

"No one."

"Call me later."

"I'll try."

"Promise."

"I'll try."

When I opened the door, Steve was hesitating at the foot of the stairs. "I've come for my things." He climbed steadily without pausing and followed me into the apartment.

"Did you hire a car?" I asked.

"No, I taxied it."

"I'll get you one."

"Don't bother."

"Please."

"I don't want a car from your Mafioso buddies to drag me off into Jersey and shoot me."

"You made your point for two years about the company I keep. Let someone come who can help us move some things."

"Yeah, and then he cases out my apartment?"

"Let's not do it this way," I pleaded.

"What way?" he snapped.

"The bitter way."

He shook his head and surveyed the bags I had begun to fill with old gifts. I called our car service to arrange for a car.

"Immediate pickup—account number seven-six-zero-nine."

At first I ignored Steve rummaging through things, but soon I found myself placing random articles in shopping bags to help clear him from my life. He was uncharacteristically grabbing at items that had no sentimental value to him, but represented my personality. He wanted the seashell frame I made in grade school because it now held a picture of us. He took my favorite beach towel and a tote bag for diving gear I had bought myself during a long weekend in Aruba. It was apparent he was collecting data to prove we were together. The same way I had categorized his body for my memory he was collecting things from my apartment to build a collage of our time together. It was sad—our memories would not hold us together, and we both searched for things to prove we had been in love.

He followed me through each room, protesting that he was entitled to more than I was shoving into each garbage bag. In just a few moments he was distracted and stopped packing as soon as I began to do it for him. I felt it was the last nice thing I could do for him and instead of rushing I took just an extra few seconds to fold what I put in each bag because I knew he would live out of them until they were all empty. I saw those bags in a few weeks' time, some bent, torn, handles pulled off on one side and well creased, pieces of his life scattered around his apartment we once shared, and it made me sad.

When he looked through the music collection for his own things, I put my good hand over his extra set of keys and slipped them into my pocket. To accomplish this I allowed him to abscond with my entire Neil Diamond collection.

When the car arrived the driver helped me load the disorganized items into the trunk as if they were my own; my wounded hand made him sympathetic. He carried bags, lamps, and a few appliances down the stairs from the apartment. As a professional driver he followed etiquette and ignored Steve, but I knew he saw him sitting on the couch muttering to himself.

There was barely enough room in the luxury car as I tried to organize the items. After several attempts to make things fit I felt my temper rising. It was just the line of resentment I could never control. Seconds ago I was tenderly packing for him with regret and yet now as I struggled to place his things neatly in the car I was furious he was sitting on the couch doing nothing but surveying the apartment. It was suddenly enough that I had helped him to pack; he could have at least put the bags in the car. Violently pushing things into the trunk, I caused one of the garbage bags to split. Shirts in dry cleaning bags, ties, socks, sneakers, shoehorns, magazines, a bedside lamp, and a clock radio spilled onto the street. Exasperated, I kicked it all together into a tight pile and threw it in the passenger seat.

I asked the driver to wait for one moment and I ran upstairs in a panic, thinking that Steve might habitually be looking for his keys. I was wrong. He was just sitting on the couch, sinking into the cushions and his confusion.

"Steve, it is time for you to leave."

He stood and held my shoulders with his large palms. I felt the heat and sweat between his fingers as he gently shook me back and forth.

"One of us will regret this moment."

It was everything I could do to remain quiet and refrain from saying "It won't be me" as I followed him out the door.

10

Ready or Not

The river that surrounds Manhattan has different qualities on each border. My East Side roots always biased me into believing that the West Side was colder. A stranger to both would argue that in the summer the breeze was enjoyable on both sides and in the winter each wind chill was unforgiving. On the West Side the new concrete parks and designer jungle gyms have given New Yorkers another place to parade themselves on the weekends. The only unfortunate side effect of Battery Park City is that more people come downtown instead of hovering above Fifty-ninth Street in Central Park.

As I walked to Zoe's house in the West Village, I wondered how friends allow one another to continue in unhealthy relationships. I suppose, it is our job to stand by and support each another. Unconditional love must come from somewhere, and for me friendship is what catches us when we fall from the graces of others.

No matter how warm the evening was, I knew Zoe would wear a leather coat or leather pants. I wore a thin leather blazer over a white T-shirt, mimicking the models I had observed all day, hoping it would look like I was in control.

"Let me in or I'll blow your house down," I screamed up to her window.

"Get up here!" she yelled back at me through the intercom.

As I reached the door I heard the scramble of paws on the hardwood floor. When we hugged, the dogs jumped on us, and a claw pierced the sleeve of my coat. Zoe was in custom French underwear, and her body was still warm from the shower. Her red hair was wet and untamed. We both spoke at once in quick bits, more like sound bites, apologies for the silences over the past few months, neither of us wanting to admit the awkwardness of judging each other.

"Talk to Emily?" I asked.

"We've spoken, but not *talked*," she sighed. "You know me." She smiled and threw her hands up in the air.

Zoe liked to mix business with pleasure. It was natural that she would marry someone she worked for. There was never a place she was employed—law firms to barrooms—that within a week she wasn't dating the owner or senior partner. I liked to compare our childhoods because a restaurant parent raised her. There was never enough time to give Zoe the attention a daughter requires from her mother. At every meal there were critics to impress, moneylenders to adore, or the general waitstaff with questions about what the entrée specials were. Zoe had become the type of woman who didn't flinch at the sight of blood and was never impressed by roses.

On the street we walked to the rhythm of her striding gait. In college I could hear her coming down the hall three rooms away;

boom, boom, swish, boom, boom, swish. The heel of her motorcycle boot hit the floor hard and the sway of her hip brought the soft pause between the crashing thunder of her steps. Zoe and I were the working class of the Ivy Leagues. At Cornell, we were up before dawn on a baking schedule, ordering vegetables, or multiplying food costs by cup and gallon measurements while the other kids were coming home from pledge parties. Once a year the Hotel School took over the dinning halls and sponsored banquets and buffets to impress the pre-med–pre-law students. No matter how well we could cook an omelette or make neat sushi rolls we were still stuck wearing polyester chef pants and cleaning up the floor after everyone else went to their next sorority meeting. Zoe and I managed to badger the bureaucracy enough so they allowed us to take a few courses in feminist literature. There we met Emily, who became our tour guide of the best professors and classes to sign up for.

We walked down to a tavern by the water. A good immigrant crowd hung out there, as well as the trendy artist types. That evening it was a very blue-collar-and-turpentine combination. The owner swooned over us a bit, and it almost felt like a homecoming. In the three hours we were together I barely had to mention Steve, because Zoe was busy elaborating on her life.

"Can you believe it? Miama Handlemen walks into your bar with an entire photography crew, and he didn't know it was her?" Zoe slammed her hand on the table. "I couldn't believe it! That's like Mapplethorpe walking into a leather store and not knowing who he is."

"She usually stands behind the camera, not in front of it," I said, surprisingly rising to Aaron's defense. Zoe was making me tired. She was so delighted with the success of the bar and the glamorous crowds it was attracting that she was denying Aaron's excessive drinking and abusive temper. It was one a.m. when we decided to taxi in opposite directions.

Zoe went to the bar to check on the crowd and I directed my taxi toward the club where the model said he would be. Just a drink, I thought. I walked a few more blocks, hoping to change my mind, but I knew I wouldn't. When I decide on taking action I rarely change my mind. There is a value to learning this way: I never make the same mistakes twice, but I usually make big mistakes.

The club had some barely pronounceable name. I marched past the velvet ropes and stared at a girl who tried to stop me. I pretended to be insulted but understanding and asked the bouncer to look for my name on the list. Ironically, I was actually on it and I did not have to act as if I was confused or pay twenty dollars to enter. I was immediately grateful I had decided to wear leather.

There was no sign of the model at the bar. Be a good girl and go home, I told myself. Instead, I walked up a set of large sweeping stairs. At the top of the foyer was another lounge where Alexander talked to three women. He was wearing a light beige suit. In my jeans I felt juvenile and I chided myself for coming at all. I leaned on the railing to watch him. He worked the entire room, making each woman feel like the center of his attention. Another good-looking man in jeans approached me. He was older, with a thinning hairline, but he had an aura that made me comfortable. He thought I was someone he knew.

"You must be Catherine," he said, extending a hand. "Alexander has been talking about you all night. My name is Alex, too. Would you like a drink?"

The other Alexander was suddenly at his side. "Are you already hitting on my date? It's good you came." He leaned down and kissed me on the cheek like an old lover.

"It looked like you were busy until now, anyway." I smiled and shrugged a shoulder in the direction of the three women, who watched us closely.

"She is a *smart* woman," said Alex.

"I've been talking about you all night—ask him—my friends were beginning to think you didn't really exist." He smiled innocently.

"I almost didn't exist. If your friend hadn't saved me I'd be hiding behind that palm tree until the place closed."

They both laughed, although a bit affected and loud.

"What about my drink?" I asked. I made eyes at the model to fetch it and for his friend to stay. For as difficult as relationships are it is amazing how easy men can be to handle.

"Don't steal this one," he said before walking away.

"What do you do, Alex?" I asked.

"I'm a conceptualist. A restaurant consultant. I used to be a chef, but I wanted out from behind the line. Basically I wanted to wear some shoes without steel toes."

"I know the feeling."

"Are you a chef?"

"No. I work in the fish market."

"Really? That is impressive."

"If you like the smell of fish."

"I do." He paused while I ignored the innuendo. "How long have you and Alexander known each other? He has nothing but the best to say about you. Why haven't we met before?"

Either the model was a weirdo or he believed in love at first sight. "We really haven't known each other for that long," I said.

"I'm glad you joined us. After everything he said about you tonight I really wanted to meet you."

"I just want to sleep with him."

Alex stepped back, finished his drink, and took out a piece of paper and a pen. "If it doesn't work out with him, can I take you out?" he asked.

I looked at my watch. "Are you free for breakfast?" I laughed. "You don't think I'd show up here at one-thirty in the morning with the intention to go home alone, do you?"

"You are everything he said you were."

Alexander was back at our side. "So what's the word?" he asked.

"Marry her," said Alex.

"I told you she was one of a kind."

"Can you really tell all that in the *short* amount of time we've known each other?" I asked.

"I've known you were special since I walked into your office." He liked giving me the feeling that this attraction had some validity by making the tension seem longer and more significant than it was.

"Why haven't we met her before?"

"I was engaged." I held up my bandaged hand.

"Looks like you still are," he said.

"I can't get the ring off until the swelling goes down."

"She's the type you fall for. Be careful," said Alex.

"You boys don't fall for anyone. The hunt is always more fun than the kill." I swallowed my drink in two impolite swigs and turned to Alexander. "Can we go now?"

They were both quiet for a moment.

"I have a morning meeting. I can't stay up all night." I gave his friend a hug and swept down the stairs. Above the music and cacophony of glasses at the bar I heard the taunting snicker of the three women who the model had abandoned to speak with me. They commented on my appearance, my height, the roundness of my face, and the fullness of my hips. I managed to keep a cool, even stride until I reached the door and was outside.

"You're pensive, aren't you?" asked Alexander, enclosing his hand in mine. I pressed my head into his chest while he kissed my neck and ears. He had smoky breath from the Scotch in his drink and a cool tongue from the ice. I wrapped myself around him, believing in his earnestness for the moment. Every man in a certain class, with a certain education, was by now becoming the same. Either they went through the Ivy Leagues, or the less fortunate ones caught up in graduate school. They were making money and they all had the same taste and the same toys. It didn't matter which Alex I went home with tonight or tomorrow night. Most of the men I was attracted to evolved into similar molds. Finding the one who was different was the challenge. I knew I had to stop playing games with the generic types in order to find him, but tonight this one would work.

When the alarm sounded I had two choices: One was to taxi home, shower, change, and then hurry back to my meeting in this neighborhood. Slightly hungover and dangerously close to throwing up, I moved too slowly to travel home and had no choice but to clean up and leave.

The most intimate peek inside someone's life after accessing his refrigerator is using his bathroom. What people keep behind their shower curtains and medicine cabinets are windows into their lives. After learning to judge a restaurant by its freezer or walk-in refrigerator, I applied the same rules to bathrooms. If a walk-in is clean, organized, and the contents are securely covered with plastic wrap, or neatly placed in sealed containers, I recommend the restaurant. If I attend a dinner party and the host's bathroom has pubic hair in the cracks of the tiles, stains in the toilet, or crusty tubes of face cream on the shelf, I refrain from eating anything that is not well done. It is a prudish and clinical way to evaluate people, but bacteria threatens most of my resources, and I am a stickler for regulation. The hypocrisy is that I'll go to bed with a complete stranger, crediting only latex as my sanitary protection.

The model's medicine cabinet was full of expensive skin treatments. I imagined that the tiny bottle of moisturizer I held cost over a hundred dollars and the heavy glass bottle almost slipped from my mitten-bandaged hand. I didn't want to make any commotion—I wanted him to keep sleeping, or just pretend he was still sleeping, so we wouldn't have to deal with awkward farewells or make promises we wouldn't keep. I showered with the plastic liner from the wastebasket around my hand to protect it from getting wet, and then pampered myself with his scrubs, creams, and hair ointments.

In the bedroom I rummaged quietly through his walk-in closet. Choosing a cream-colored pinpoint cotton shirt that dressed up my jeans and loafers, I would promise to drop it off with the doorman some other time. Somewhere inside, I knew already that it was my trophy for the night.

Before he even rolled over and made morning grunts, I was in the kitchen sipping the coffee I had made. I heard the daily paper settle outside the door, the thick sections spreading lightly on the mat. Toying with the fantasy of commitment, I imagined the apartment belonged to me and my lover as I brought the paper inside. Glancing through the headlines, lamenting at the awful news, I wondered how our children would ever grow up in this world.

With a deep sigh of relief, I laid the paper aside, rinsed my cup, and looked around the kitchen for a piece of paper to write him a short note about his shirt. There were two stacks of thick legal text and no scraps. Unable to deny myself the trespass, I skimmed the written material. The first page was the terms of agreement concerning his divorce. I didn't really understand it all except that the divorce would be final four months from now. Technically I just slept with a married man and he slept with a woman still wearing her engagement ring. It was hard to decide if the situation was humorous or pathetic, but it was easy to decide against a note.

The elevator man smiled with knowing closed lips, and I properly ignored him. The early-morning heat made me self-conscious in my leather coat. Across the street a woman strolled behind her dog in an old pair of sneakers, sweatpants, and a light sweater. Disgust settled into my morning. I wanted to exchange places, because I knew she lived the fantasy. She was out on a warm morning walk with her dog before she returned home to a fluffy couch and drank decaffeinated coffee all day. Her loving husband was on his way to work at a bank, and her children were enrolled in a competitive private school. Her days were filled with small things: lunches, dry cleaning, laundry, and the security of sloppy kisses from her thankful dog and children. Her country house was covered in old blankets and some strange crotchet pillows her deaf aunt made in the seventies. It was a dreadful moment on the street corner—here was my status as a single woman, being dragged toward thirty, raw in the crotch from an endless night of acrobatic sex, wearing someone else's clothes to my meeting, and possibly buying a pair of underwear at the drugstore so that the seam in my jeans didn't irritate me. I was jealous because life at the end of a cul-de-sac works for some women, and just for a moment I wished I were one of them.

The restaurant was still dark when I arrived and slipped into the bathroom to check my appearance. It was exactly how I remembered—underdressed, oversize clothes, slightly tired, and handsome in a disheveled way. I turned the light off and entered the dark room where voices filled only a portion of the space. I have a fondness for closed restaurants. One that is quiet, void of people and the energy that it takes to make it operate, has a certain holiness, like a church before Saturday Mass.

"What do you think of the bathroom?" asked Jake, a senior investor who owns pieces of six other restaurants in Manhattan.

"Great full-length mirror—but of course, you know what that means?" I asked.

Jake looked up at me. "The tables won't turn fast enough because the women will congregate in the bathroom?"

I nodded and seated myself.

"I thought it was good to have a full-length mirror," said Kevin, an ex-actor junior investor who did well for himself and wanted to open his own restaurant before his career failed. The concept was a traditional fishy dive with exquisite cuisine. There would be whale sounds and Captain Hook memorabilia.

"It could be risky. Diet control for the Mannorexics." I smiled.

"Mannorexics?" Kevin squinted his face.

Jake put his hand over mine and tapped it lightly. "She means Manhattan anorexics. A certain type of wealthy woman with an eating disorder. The rich and starving for attention." Jake smiled.

Kevin seemed very distressed at the thought of people not eating.

"Don't worry, Kevin. Just make sure you have a good bar." I poured coffee into my cup and Jake pushed his toward me to fill it.

George, the chef, brought fresh-baked muffins and a platter of soft scrambled eggs to the table. We have known each other and have slept together at various times for about six years. When we met, he was fresh out of the Culinary Institute and I was just a recent addition to my father's business. He had had a good medicine cabinet, lots of natural herbal shampoos. Seeing each other like this made us remember we've both gotten somewhere, wherever that is.

"Nice shirt," said George. "Looks about my size." He knew I liked trophies, and well-crafted oxford shirts were my favorite.

Street noise entered the building, a siren, a car honk, standard screeching, and then the door closed again and it was quiet.

"Hope we didn't hold you all up." Apologetically, Sid Niceman bowed his head.

I've slept with Sid, too; he is quite a bit older but a perpetual flirt and charmer. I always found him an easy man to be around. We have the same refrigerator idiosyncrasies and similar Rolodexes; there was a time when I thought we could be happily married. Ironically, I'm too old for him now. He likes the girls very young and very uninformed, especially about him.

"You know Sid Niceman, of course," said Jake.

"Of course." I nodded, rose from my seat, and shook hands.

"This is Alex Craft. He's going to be our creative consultant, all-around kind of man."

Without hesitation I met eyes with the model's friend. "Alex and I have crossed paths just recently."

All men were now falling into the category that single women hate to admit exists; old women with too many bags hiss it, mothers in grocery stores stand between the aisles and whisper it, and any hairdresser will tell you before they've washed out your roots. All men become the same.

Alex smiled and nodded. I looked around the table. The delicate dance of sex for the successful businesswoman is a balancing act no one wants to discuss. There is the legal jargon and harassment law but there are no rules about business and pleasure. There are only tests. I'm regarded with high esteem at these meetings, even though I usually say very little and agree with the others, because I have managed to fornicate without attachment.

Alex talked about publicity and Kevin jumped in with Hollywood names, overdoing it with grandeur. He was a kid without training wheels, reckless. Jake soothed him, threw him a flattering biscuit, and then talked about whom to hire for the interior. They came up with a list of ten designers, threw five out immediately. They threw another out for remembering what a lousy job he did with a place in California—and then put him back on the list because it was really "not his territory." These meetings were actually very boring, but I feigned interest because this was a big project and it was better than being at my desk. It would mean an increase in general net profits for the year because the restaurant would showcase exotic fish and demand a constant flow of fresh imports. Exquisite fish die so easily, it would be revolving cash for their constant demand.

"You've been quiet, Cece. What about your two bits?" asked Alex.

"More like sixty bits to every man's dollar." I smiled and took a sip of my coffee. "That goes for the women who don't get big diamonds." I reached for one of my favorite muffins.

Sid gently patted the thick bandages. "It seems, my dear, you had your chance." My father must have forewarned the team here today because no one was surprised by my hand.

"I have to give it back once the swelling goes down." I looked down at the growing yellow stains and blue bruising; then I practiced tapping my fingers on the table like the doctor said.

Jake gave me quick condolences and for a moment the table was at a loss for words.

"When did it happen?" asked Alex. A question I never answered the night before.

"My fiancé called off our wedding, and when I was holding him down to stab him with the ice pick it went through my hand instead."

Everyone but Kevin and Alex laughed.

Sid smiled affectionately. In the beginning when my father and I argued over small things, unlike now when we argue over the big things, my father asked Sid to keep an eye on me; Sid had added his hands.

"Did you sleep last night?" Sid asked. There was a question and it was my turn to respond, but in my head I was packing for my honeymoon.

"Excuse me, I'm taking mental notes. I'm working on some combinations for the opening party, but I need to check their spawning seasons."

"Come back from the big blue and tell us what you think of Perry for interior design." There was a warning tone in Sid's voice that only I could recognize. He was trying to tell me that someone at this table is related to Perry, had slept with Perry, is sleeping with Perry, had worked with Perry, hates him, or loves him. Sid's tone said: Tread lightly.

"Randy Perry?"

"Cor-rect." Jake was cautionary.

"He did a nice job of the Madness Café. He's great for period pieces and really does his homework. Nice touch on claw feet for everything in Big Tubs Bar and Grill. It depends on what type of authenticity you want or if you're leaning toward a touch of camp."

"All that from the lady who claims she only knows fish." Sarcasm laced with a compliment from Alex.

Maybe Kevin and Randy Perry were an item. Like all the Hollywood beauties, maybe he's not straight but he doesn't want his female fan club to know. I sighed and gave them each an earnest, intense look eye to eye.

"The ball is really for Alex. He is the visionary and only he can know who can help bring it all together for you. At this point it is really a chemistry thing. All the designers you've named know their business. Perry has the right sense of balance—good on realism and able to throw in a touch of the dream sequence. I think he can keep it modern without getting hokey. Class with no kitsch," I added.

There were a few nodding heads.

Sid reached into his briefcase. "We need to discuss some financial organization."

"If you gentlemen don't mind, I'm going to check out the foyer and see what kinds of tanks the foundation can hold."

No one made it easy for me to exit the banquette, and I brushed their laps with my ass.

The foyer was directly in front of the bar and formed a semicircle behind the host stand. If you were in the dining room, you couldn't see out; if the bar was crowded with people, you couldn't see in. Kevin obviously expected big talent to be regulars and wanted to hide them from their best enemy: fans. The bar provided a natural barrier from the dining room. To people-watch, you needed to buy a drink. It did limit where tanks could be placed, and their expense might be enormous because they should stand from floor to ceiling. I never like window tanks on the street because it makes fish nervous. Like any sane creature, eventually the city creeps in and begins to wear on them.

Sid was breathing on my neck. "Aren't you pensive about business today?" He gave me a small bite on the ear before stepping away.

"I want the contract. Can you blame me? If he has any type of success—and he should with George in the kitchen, the whole thing could do a lot for the business."

"Your father never relied on trendy."

"*Really?* You should see what kind of crap consulting we're doing now for travel magazines. It was a different city then. He had clients that had restaurants that stayed alive for decades. The Quilted Giraffe closed. What the hell is next? Tavern on the Green? Nobody goes to the institutions anymore except to see some old-timer. Everything has got to be new. People barely sit down before they decide to go somewhere else for dessert." I sighed, realizing how tired I sounded.

Sid smiled and put his arm around my shoulder. "I love you most when you're like this. Serious, hungry to make your own success." He paused. "I'm sorry about Steve."

"Me, too."

"I better get back. What are you doing tonight?"

"Waxing my legs and going to bed early."

* * *

A Las Vegas mermaid would be great for the opening party, a beautiful girl who breathes through a tube and swims around performing tricks.

"Catherine?" Kevin's hesitant chirp.

"Call me Cece, please. Want to talk about mermaids?"

"Will they grant wishes?"

"Don't you know that real mermaids are like women? They just need some guy to help them acquire feet. Then for sure they'll use those feet to walk away."

"Is that why no one pulls them from the sea anymore?" he asked playfully.

"Mermaids were too much work, and now men are hooked on mail-order brides from Asia and the Ukraine."

"I just wanted to say thanks for your honesty concerning Randy. I was in a bind. You really helped me out." He looked at the floor. "My brother and Randy have this thing going on."

"I had no idea." I smiled. "Randy has talent. You shouldn't worry about what people say. You're almost a New York restaurateur! Big glamour. A lot of women!" I punched him lightly in the gut.

"Had it in Los Angeles."

"I forgot you're already a star. You just need the restaurant to keep up your acid face-scrub schedule and chin-lifts." I wondered if my mouth could ever slow down long enough to listen to my brain.

"Do you always say what's on your mind?"

"Unfortunately. Sorry."—and I truly was.

"I guess you would never lie to me?" he asked, stepping into my personal space.

"Only to get what I want." *All men are the same,* I repeated in my head. I took his hand and held it for a flirtatious moment. He was good-looking in the synthetic sort of way. "You had better go back to them—they might think you're more interested in fish food than making money. That makes them nervous."

"Leave me a message about getting together next week. You and Randy can discuss the theme." He winked and did a little dance as he turned away. I recognized it from a movie he was in.

George came my way via the kitchen. We barely spoke. He and I stood facing the room and put our arms around one another's waists. Like kids going back for a high-school reunion, we felt old together. The transition from lover to friend was not easy, but he is one of my most important friends who honestly reflect my past. We fight the urge to pretend we could make it as a couple, but there is a lovely feeling that comes over me when I'm with him. We like the same things, enjoy good food, a fast joke, and the sex was great.

"Are we thinking the same thing?" he asked.

"I suppose, but let's not ruin it by actually saying it out loud. I'm not too strong right now, and I'd like to pretend there is something for me to look forward to."

"Maybe there is."

"I don't want to destroy much more in my callow youth." I smiled, using an expression that my mother often used when I was being headstrong.

"You mean there might be hope after our second marriage falls through?"

"Let me just make it to my first." We hugged for a moment.

George stiffened. "Cece? Why do you think you eat men alive? Its like you've got something against them. They get tossed into your life, and once you've got them past the fear of a relationship you throw them into the *cuisine-heart.*"

"*Cuisine-heart?* What are you, a chef?"

"That wasn't an engagement. That was Steve's death wish."

I shut my eyes and George hugged me again before returning to the kitchen. I felt sick. Too much coffee, not enough sleep, too much talking about Steve, not enough me to go around.

Alex approached me. He came out of the dark, sharing a secret in his grin, and kissed me lightly on the cheek. "You didn't mention *where* you had a meeting in the morning. I thought you were just using that to get home last night."

"I don't need excuses." I crossed my arms over my chest.

"What really happened to your hand?"

"I smashed it on a message spike."

"And the part about your fiancé?"

"All true. He moved out yesterday."

"You bounce back pretty fast," he said.

"Everyone needs to break the spell."

"When can I see you?"

"In a month or so, if I'm still doing Alex's. I'm taking a vacation down in the islands, but I'll be back before they make any real decisions."

"I've done a lot of scuba diving in the Caribbean. Where are you going?"

"St. John."

"It has some good spots for snorkeling—there are places nearby that have exquisite underwater parks."

"If there is sun and rum, any island is good for a honeymoon spent alone."

11

Solemnly Swear

If August is a lady in the evening, during the day she is a bitch. The sun was high and hot by the time I left the restaurant. My leather jacket and oversize shirt were a ridiculous combination in the sudden heat. I walked down Fifth Avenue by the trendy expensive shops that had multiplied above Fourteenth Street.

A slick pair of alligator loafers caught my attention. When I turned toward the window I lost my balance and slipped on the rubber mats being washed outside. For a moment I almost writhed around on the cool wet mats playing with a makeshift slip'n slide, a favorite childhood game to cool off in the city heat. I was feeling so ridiculous in my soaked jeans and heavy jacket that I jogged all the way down the avenue, breaking a heavy sweat.

My breath was short and my legs were tired when I arrived at Washington Square Park. I hailed a taxi and watched the city pass by as I made my way back downtown. From the seaport almost everything but the financial district is "uptown." When the

South Street Seaport underwent construction it was unbearable at first. An invasion of investors, builders, and architects created a walkway of cute shops and tourist venues. Eventually the eye adjusted to the new population: tourists and suits who joined the bloodstained smocks and old rubber boots. It was a movement that was hard to stop; not only had the seaport lost its flare in New York, but Little Italy was gentler, the Upper West Side was trendy, and TriBeCa was no longer barren.

When I entered the office Chelsea had her arms folded across her chest and lips pursed in disapproval. Six men sat in the waiting area. They were not models, but could have been. They still dressed in black jeans and leather and had very good hair.

"Hi, I have a meeting with—a Miss—I think she said it was Lacey?" I asked with my head down.

"She's been having problems with Hong Kong," snapped Chelsea. We always use Hong Kong as a fake reference when we're trying to discuss something private in public. "Ms. Lacey told me that if you wanted to look at the apartment for rent I could bring you upstairs."

"Oh, great! Thanks a lot."

Chelsea tells the men waiting it shouldn't be too much longer since I just reached my customs contact. On the way up the stairs I began to strip down.

"Did you have enough coffee yet?" She smiled, sitting down on the couch to have a cigarette.

I dropped my wet jeans. "Where's my father?" I asked.

"Not coming today. He said he would be here Thursday by lunch so you could head down to Pennsylvania after your doctor's appointment." Chelsea sat up a little straighter and evaluated the empty spaces on the coffee table. "What's missing?" she asked.

"Steve's things."

"*He* already called."

I spun around, naked, and stared at her in disbelief. "Who called?"

"The model guy from yesterday. You know I never forget a voice. A face sure, but never a voice."

"I thought you meant Steve called."

"He did, too. I just thought it was more interesting that the model guy called."

Flattered, I skipped into the other room.

"No skipping! We've got a hell of a day and you're going to hate me by five o'clock. Now hustle," she yelled after me.

On our way down the stairs I spoke in two voices, my own and the imaginary girl looking to rent a room. Chelsea interrupted us, swung open the door and we both pretended to wave good-bye.

"Nice girl. Don't you think, Chelsea?" I asked as we entered the room full of photographers.

"She seemed a bit young. The kind who likes to stay out all night."

I smiled. "Better to stay out all night than to make noise at home."

"Good point." She extended her hand and waved it about the office. "We have some work to do."

"Who's first?" I held the door to my office open.

The first group was easy to dismiss because they used stark lighting and shadows for effect, and it made everything appear as if it were rising from the dead. I staggered through the next few interviews, asking the correct questions, but was unimpressed. The last agent I saw was Eddie, who had deep inset eyes, hazelnut-colored hair, and a calculated but shy drop to his chin. The photographer was Argentinean, Miguel, and he spoke with such a heavy accent I could barely understand him. All the work contained in his portfolio had a soothing tropical style. There was a lazy background feeling that emitted heat. Even if waiting had made them impatient, they were polite and professional. I flipped through his portfolio several times, enjoying the entire essence of the images; it was not until my third time through the pictures that I noticed a photo of the model I slept with last night. They had been watching my expression carefully.

"Something you like?" asked Miguel in his thick cloudy accent.

"Someone I know." I smiled to myself.

"That is Alexander! We're good friends. He stays with me when he works out on the West Coast. How do you know him?"

"I'm a friend of his ex-wife's." I smiled. "Could I interest you gentlemen in lunch? It is purely seafood and salads around here, but I know the best places for both."

The agent's eyes lit up. We're both contract seekers, and lunch is a sign that things are going well.

"Chelsea?"

"Yes?"

"How about some lunch? The usual for us and order two more. Find out what came in this morning from Frank. Please, no salmon, only tuna or grouper. Tell them it's for me. Some bubble water, too."

Eddie gave me a hard look. He was too good-looking to be a puppy-dog type but too small to avoid being called boyish. The photographer was a bit manlier, but he also had a boyish quality that made me think they would enjoy building sand castles.

"Do you like sand castles?" I asked them.

"What?" They looked at each other.

"Sand castles? I mean with all those locations, beaches, coastlines, you must do a lot of sitting around. I figured you were probably good at building sand castles."

"Girls make sand castles. Boys dig holes."

"I thought dogs did that?" I said, and both of them smiled.

While we waited for lunch Miguel looked through his own portfolio, which proved how much he liked his own work. "This is one of my favorites," he said.

It was a beach scene with great landscapes of the body and wet expensive clothes clinging to the models in the sea. The women appeared glamorous and relaxed, stunning and feminine, strong and soft.

"Wish it was me," I sighed.

"Aren't you leading the trip?"

"No, that's a story that seems to have grown out in the waiting room. I'm just mapping out the itinerary and making suggestions for real sport fishing."

"Any diving?" asked Eddie.

"Everyone loves diving today," I said, exasperated. "Are they paying the agent to travel?"

"Rarely, I just like to use the hotel room. That is, of course, if you decide to work with us?" Eddie bearned flirtatiously.

"*If* I decide to work with you? I only make suggestions. The last word belongs to Tulley."

"But it is weight," said Miguel.

His grammatical error made me smile.

"I know what it is!" said Eddie.

"What?" I asked.

"I've seen you somewhere before."

"And?"

"You're getting married. I saw the photograph this weekend."
He came close to patting himself on the back.

Chelsea buzzed me.

"Lunch?" I said, almost gasping.

"Him."

"Which him?"

"It's Steve."

"I'm not taking the call. What could he want to talk about?"

"The ring."

Chelsea was exasperated. I was sure her facade was crumbling the more calls she fielded about the cancellation of the wedding. I pushed the ball of my hand into my eye sockets to stop an oncoming headache.

"Please, please, Chelsea, just get rid of him."

"We're closing the office as soon as lunch is over."

"Anything, anything, I just can't talk to him right now."

I rubbed my eyes hard until I saw green, burgundy, pink, and purple splotches.

"I'm a little grumpy when I don't eat." They nodded in unison. "I feel comfortable that you won't alienate the men I rely on. As far as I'm concerned, the job is yours. With that said, I can now write our lunch off." I stretched and sat back into my large leather chair.

In my office, with the seedy smell of diesel and rotting fish, I was in control for just a moment.

All day Wednesday Chelsea and I organized the office, listed appointments, made notes, and evaluated what could go wrong while I was on vacation and prepared as much as possible for disasters we didn't expect. When we locked up the office it was early and I was completely drained.

To take a proper shower, and prevent water from saturating

my bandages, I wrapped my hand in a plastic bag and taped the edges to my wrist. I had almost spun the silver duct tape around my wrist when it slipped off the edge of the bag and fell to the floor. As I searched around for the roll I noticed that Steve had left behind a sprinkling of pubic hair on the bathroom tiles.

The intimate remains of him in my life irritated me. I wanted to erase his presence altogether and rewind the years I had been with him in order to cleanse myself of the embarrassment. I ran into the kitchen, kept my hand wrapped in the bag, and filled two buckets with bleach and lemon-fresh disinfectant: a deadly combination if I inhaled too much. Brushing lint, dried lettuce, and torn corks onto the floor, I scrubbed down cans of tuna, peas, corn, instant soups, and beans. Everything was cleansed of dusty supermarket residue and sticky price tags. I rearranged the shelves and created separate piles for vegetables, pastas, sauces, and soups.

I opened the shelves that held dishes, cups, glasses, and old plastic beer cups that Steve collected at football games and sporting events. I loaded each dish into the automatic washer and scrubbed every nook with extra bleach before the fumes started to choke me.

A large garbage bag was attached to my jean loops by several clothespins. In the bathroom I scoured the sink, toilet, and shower, watching globs of hair and urine stains disappear. I threw out a can of shaving balm, athlete's foot powder, a razor, a bar of antiperspirant, a nose-hair clipper, a tube of hemorrhoid cream, and a thin comb from an airline kit. While the glass shelves from the medicine cabinet were soaking in a tub of bleach, I tried on any old makeup and then threw it away.

In the bedroom I found outdated condoms, personal lubricant, and a small stack of girlie magazines in between the mattress and the box spring. Each woman on the cover had huge breasts and a flawless buckskin ass. I flipped through them casually, both amazed and horrified. Each model had small tufts of perfectly shaped triangles of pubic hair or none at all. The more I inspected the photographs, the more unjust I felt it was to try to live up to the images. It was actually far worse; now when I dated men I'd wonder if every one wanted a shaved anus and inflated bronze tits. With a shudder I tossed all the magazines in the bag, unable to put them into the recycling for people to steal or leave lying around in front of my door.

In the living room I turned on the stereo and danced around to Aretha Franklin's greatest hits. I opened a bottle of wine and was careful not to get any of the cork on the now pristine Formica counter. Singing at the top of my lungs I threw pillows in the air, tossed away every aging sports section of the newspaper, and scoured the shelves where Steve had left gaping holes in my music collection. After alphabetizing the compact discs, vacuuming in between each sofa cushion, and washing the air conditioner screen, I sat down and wondered what to do with the four large volumes of wedding etiquette books and magazines that had collected an unusual amount of dust.

First, I spread the bridal magazines on one corner of the coffee table. Then I stacked them on top of one another in order of size. Just for fun I inverted the pile to see if it could stand; when it immediately fell over I celebrated by pouring myself another glass of wine. I stacked the books and the magazines, trying to remember which ones I had purchased first and why. Where did I get the idea to wear a dress when I own one skirt and hate anything with lace or embroidery? I turned the pages of each magazine quickly, searching for the patterns, ideas, and concepts that I had derived from some cute article or photograph, and then adapted to my life. I tore out folded, dog-eared, marked pages until the magazines were split at the seams and falling apart. I wrote Steve's name on the tear sheets in black Magic Marker and cut them into shreds chanting, "Set me free." I laughed and danced around the pieces singing, "You don't own me!" When I realized I had to pee I pulled down my jeans and squatted over the shredded pictures. I laughed so hard at the thought of urinating on the pile that I fell over onto my side and spilled my glass of wine on them instead.

On my way back from the bathroom I decided not to tear apart the wedding books. Perhaps I would need them someday, and the thought alone made me realize that for all of my toughness, my brawny barroom slang and loose behavior, someday I still wanted to get married. To make room on the bookshelf I threw away six volumes of pulp fiction written for lawyers by other lawyers. I sat down in Steve's favorite chair and admired my work. The apartment was clean and almost rid of his scent. The small pile of soaked magazine pages was the only trace of disorder.

A man with manicured nails is no good for a woman who cleans her own toilet. A woman who has worked herself out of yellow wading trousers into suits cannot be with a man who turned eighteen and received a stock portfolio. Passions and differences create excitement, but something different should never be confused for something permanent, and at the same time something that fits should never be confused with something that works.

"Hello," I said into the dark room as I clambered for the phone.

"Asleep?" asked Susan.

"No, yeah, I'm not sure."

"Should I call back?"

"No, no. I was housecleaning and I sat down to rest for a moment. I guess I fell asleep."

"You're coming down tomorrow, right?"

"As soon as I'm done having my hand checked at the doctor. About one o'clock."

"Good. Can you bring Brittany?"

"Huh? College? Boston? Lesbian?"

"Yeah, but do you always have to say that?" asked Susan.

"I'm just qualifying. Location, personality, how she knows you."

"Well, she doesn't know me like *that*."

"Can she meet me here?"

"She doesn't know New York that well."

"Tell her to take a cab."

"Can't you pick her up at the train station?"

"Susan, that is insanity. Midtown? I'm going to be stuck in traffic for hours."

"*Please*—her girlfriend just broke up with her."

"Don't you mean *life partner?*" I asked sarcastically.

"Obviously not anymore."

"Ugh. What time does her train get in?"

"One-forty-two from Boston."

"Tell her to follow the sign for Twisters Donuts. I'll be there."

"Hey, why don't you guys share a hotel room?"

"Why?"

"Her girlfriend isn't coming and your ex-whatever isn't coming. Why don't you share a room since you're booked at the same hotel?"

"I'm tired and cranky, but I have the distinct feeling this is not just a penny-saving idea," I said.

"*What* do you mean?"

"Remember when I came to see you in the junior class play? You had some lines about the stars and had to walk across the stage."

"Yeah."

"You're still a lousy actress, Susan."

There was a long silence and deep breath. "I just don't want either of you to be alone. Neither of you are the type of woman who will ask for help, and you're both a little frail right now."

"I'll pick her up at the station, I'll share a room, I'll be nice, but I won't spill my guts and cry on her shoulder."

"Are you mad I said you're frail?"

"No. I just want to get off the phone."

"Hey, don't forget to pack a sarong."

"What?"

"The long skirt-wrap thing we bought in Mexico. Tomorrow night's bachelorette party has a tropical Asian theme."

"You aren't supposed to know that."

"Yeah, but my sister can't keep a secret." And that, I knew, was true.

"I won't forget my sarong," I sighed.

"I love you," she said earnestly.

"No matter what I am?" I asked.

"Don't be a tease."

"I'll see you tomorrow."

I cleaned up the wet magazines and poured disinfectant on the floor. The ink from writing Steve's name had spread and created a large abstract stain on the wood that needed to be scrubbed out. I put clean sheets on the bed and organized my closet by color. On the chair I laid out several outfits and pieces I could wear this weekend, along with some ideas for my honeymoon trip. I considered packing, but my hand was puckered and sweating from being inside the bag for so long. The doctor would lecture me tomorrow, but I did not want to return to an apartment that had traces of Steve or our life together. I set the alarm early so I could go to Tiffany and have the ring cut off before I saw the doctor. Regardless of the platinum band, I was sure the jewel could be saved.

My mother was quietly moving around my apartment before the alarm went off on Thursday morning. I smelled coffee and her lilac perfume above the bleach. The clothes that I had laid out on my chair were packed into two suitcases. It was a generous gesture for them to arrive early, but I worried that my father was downstairs rampaging the office.

"Mom?"

She poked her head in my room. "Coffee?"

"Yeah, but I'll get up."

"No, no, stay in bed."

I fluffed up my pillows and looked out the window. The day was clear and sharp. The heat would be unbearable by noon. Driving into the heart of steamy Pennsylvania was not my idea of an easy way to pass the day. I let out a deep sigh.

"Tired?" asked my mother.

"Very."

She handed me a cup of coffee and sat in the chair near the corner of the bed.

"Are my clothes in there?" I pointed to the bags.

"The smaller one is for the weekend and the bigger one is for the honeymoon. When you get to the airport, leave the weekend bag in the trunk."

"Mom, I appreciate the display of affection—and I did not feel like packing—but are you sure you remembered everything?"

"Whatever I forgot you could buy."

"Where's my bridesmaid dress?"

"In a garment bag with that print scarf."

"Sarong," I corrected her. "Doesn't the house look clean?"

"Spotless. It also stinks like bleach. Did you have a cleaning frenzy?"

"Just sort of '*washing that man right out of my hair.*'"

She laughed uncomfortably.

"What? Something is bothering you. What is it?" I asked.

"Just thoughtful."

"You want to say something. What is it?"

"Nothing," she snapped.

We were silent. I waited and watched the sun over the water. When the glare was blinding I rose from bed. "I need the address of the safety deposit box for the ring," I said, walking into the kitchen.

"Your hand still looks swollen."

"I'm having it cut off."

"The whole hand?"

"Full amputation as soon as I get dressed."

"It's six in the morning. Only us fishmongers are awake."

"I'm going to wait outside Tiffany and beg to have the ring cut."

"What's the rush?" she asked, following me to the kitchen.

"My relationship is over, and I don't want to wear it. I don't care if the band is ruined. I'll give him back the jewel and he can have it reset. I don't want to bring my *ex-engagement ring* on my *ex-honeymoon.*"

"Do you want some breakfast?" she asked.

"No, I'm fine!"

"Don't scream at me because you're tired."

"I'm not screaming. You're treating me like the child I never was. You never packed for me, made me breakfast, or worried about my doctor's appointments."

"You were always my child. I was just afraid to be your mother."

"I grew up like some estranged dock boy because you were afraid to be my mother?"

"Yes."

"What the hell were you afraid of?" I tried not to yell. I looked down at my coffee. "Forget it," I said.

"I have something to say," she said.

"This is not a good time." I stood up and went into the living room. My mother remained at my heels.

"You will listen now. I want you to stop blaming me for giving you so little attention as a child."

"Mom?"

"I'm drained from watching you believe all your attributes are faults."

"You're deranged," I said, and went into the bedroom to get dressed.

"Stop running from me. All you ever wanted was a straight answer, and you're about to get it."

I stopped and stared at my mother.

"When my mother died, I swore I would never love like that again."

"Well you did a good job," and immediately I knew it was something I would regret for a very long time.

"If you were a boy it would have been different. When your father and I met, we fell in love because we recognized each other's suffering. We were different than the others in our neighborhood. We wanted more from this life, and they made us feel guilty for it. We were estranged in our community because I chose to have one child and I damn well didn't feel I had to sacrifice everything about myself as a woman once I became a mother."

In the slivers of my memory I could also see my grandfather watching my parents with distrustful wizened eyes, tracking their movements as they waited for him to die.

"You seem to think your father and I don't love each other. We know each other better than you'll ever understand. Our generation was about compromise. We went to work; we fed our children and our parents. We waited for wars to consume our systems. We were happy to have food without stealing it."

"So I should have married Steve because he and I would have a nice secure little life at the country club?"

"No, but you have to stop believing there is a perfect relationship out there waiting for you. Things are harder then you think in relationships."

"If I give up that idea that there is someone perfect I might as well call Steve before we lose the reservation at the wedding hall."

"Cece, I don't think Steve was the right person for you, but I do think you are searching for something that doesn't exist."

"Mom, just because you settled doesn't mean I have to."

Her eyes filled with anger before she yelled: "How can you live with such illusions when I raised you to be so practical!"

"Mom, you left me alone, you didn't raise me."

"I let you figure things out. I allowed you the space to become your own person and all you ever do is complain I wasn't there shoving my values down your throat. Would you have liked my father? My father was the highly righteous, religious, God-fearing son of a bitch that strangled me with his opinions. He was a man who sat me down every night and slapped my face every time I missed a word in a prayer."

"I'm sorry. I didn't mean what I said about you settling."

"Yes, you did, Cece. I know you. I wish just once you could see what we did for you. We made sure you could stand on your own two feet. We made sure you knew how to argue for yourself, defend your own opinions, and most of all to think for yourself. What surprised us is how often you felt abandoned."

"If you taught me to speak up against anything I found oppressive, then why can't you understand why I didn't marry Steve?"

She took a long deep breath and let her shoulders fall deeper into the disappointment of her aging body. "Pumpkin, I'm glad you fight back. I just want you to stop hanging on to the fairy tale that there is a Prince Charming. Your idea of relationships is unrealistic. All men make mistakes, all women make mistakes, we are imperfect, we make the wrong choices, and then we try and fix them through alcohol, shopping, lying, affairs, or by imposing our beliefs upon our children."

My mother was defeated. She had obviously believed that only princes were perfect. What she did not understand was that she had taught me exactly what she always wanted. Although I waited for the perfect fit to my strange requirements and idiosyncrasies I did not expect that it would make the man infallible.

I looked up at my mother and saw her as the woman I had liked for the past few weeks. She was funny, smart, intelligent, and charming. She had made me laugh when I was upset. The woman who I had come to know as my mother during the time my engagement disintegrated was the one I would have chosen all along.

The one I liked had made me beer and eggs for breakfast and forced me to go out to dinner when the wedding was canceled. She had called when Steve moved out and came to help pack my bags for the weekend. The mother who believed in flaws was the one I liked. If I was to ever grow up I had to see my parents for who they really were, and she was standing in front of me.

"Mom, I'm glad you let me figure out who I was without a lot of interference."

My mother wrapped her long thin muscular arms around my shoulders and rocked me slowly.

12

Cold Hands, Warm Heart

After I had unwrapped my hand, the gentleman at the Tiffany counter turned my hand back and forth under a mining-light microscope worn on his head. If I looked into the crystal source of light, his eye bulged like a frog's from its socket. He was in the middle of a long speech about the importance of the ring's design when I noticed a well-suited man hovering near us. The suited man requested we join him in a private sitting room upstairs.

"What is he here for?" I asked.

"Witness," said the jewel appraiser.

The room was filled with a simple conference table and elaborate chairs with false Elizabethan embroidery. It was as if someone had ordered a comfortable office chair to be reupholstered in a mock sixteenth-century fabric.

The well-suited man spoke. "I must explain the legal aspect of our confinements in regard to your request. Let me—"

"You're a lawyer, right?" I asked.

"Correct. Let me introduce—"

"I don't care what the legal aspects are, and I don't care if the ring explodes into tiny slivers of glass that embed themselves into my eye."

"You must understand we are under no obligation to remove the ring even though it was purchased here," said the lawyer coldly.

"*You* must understand that I am an angry woman with very little patience for your political agenda." I was beginning to understand why people had an overall dislike for lawyers.

"We at Tiffany and Company have no agenda. We merely remain loyal to our customers." He twitched his nose and shut his eyes quickly so I would not notice how he shifted his gaze to the floor. Only a good liar catches a bad one, and I caught him. Steve was obviously the customer they were loyal to. He had been here and forewarned Tiffany not to cut the ring. It was a lapse on my part not to have clearly understood that the arrangements for the diamond's safety box were at the bank across the street. The two men watched me closely as I sat back in my chair and took a deep breath.

"There must be someone else I can talk to," I said.

"I'm afraid—"

"I'm not. Get me someone else."

Both men left the room, making low breathy noises of dissatisfaction. I began to sort through a small black velvet pencil case next to a magnifying glass that sat in the corner of the room like a manicurist's table. There were sharp surgical supplies that looked like tools a dentist would use. Picks, spoons, scoops, baby pliers, little files, knives, and a sharp baby saw were offering themselves to me, begging to be used. I glanced at the open door, where a disinterested guard stood and quietly wheeled the tool table around to my right.

The heat had swollen my finger on the way here, but the crisp air-conditioned rooms lured moisture from my body into the vents, and the ring was cold. I slipped my finger into my mouth and slobbered around the setting.

I closed my eyes and thought of all the magazines I had thrown out last night, the ones Steve had collected between the mattresses. As my internal heat grew, I thought about asking the jeweler to leave when he and the lawyer returned; then I thought about sliding my hand along the lawyer's thigh while he talked distractedly in legal jargon, allowing my grip to rest on his member and feel it swell, imagining myself mounting him in the royal office chair . . . I stuck my hand into my pants and deep into the stirring between my legs. My finger warmed with wetness while I steadily watched the door. I could hear the chanting soft mantra of women's voices answering the phones for catalog sales. I removed my fingers carefully from my underpants and slid the small jagged saw between the moist finger and the ring. My hand left a sticky mark on the polished table. I worked the saw back and forth, creating a steady friction. Beads of sweat formed on my upper lip, and my right hand cramped around the tiny tool. A small slit opened on the band that provided me with enough room to wiggle the ring up to my knuckle. Sharp pain shot through my forearm when I tried to push it farther.

Someone passed by the door without even looking in. The beauty of being in an executive conference room was the feigned, polite ignorance of my existence by the rest of the staff. The guard must have heard my grunts, but it was his job to be discreet and avoid eye contact.

I imagined having to wear the ring until the hand had completely healed. The small sliver I had sawed away pinched and the pressure drew blood away from the skin below my knuckle. I didn't want to think of Steve, but I did. I wasn't angry at him, just at what had passed between us, and my fury was at myself because I always had the option to confront him and avoided it. I hated more than anything how harshly I judged myself and in God's eyes begged to be free from my self-dissatisfaction. I wanted to love my wildness and independence and stop loathing its effects. Rocking back and forth I began to chant Thou shalt not hate, thou shalt not hate, thou shalt not hate, thou shalt not hate.

As I tugged down on the thin flesh of my finger with baby tweezers, tiny bits of skin moved under the band. To distract myself from the pain I yelled at the top of my lungs *"Thou shalt not hate! Thou shalt not hate! Thou shalt not hate!"* When I finally jimmied the ring over the knuckle, the excruciating ache was a joy. Throbbing, circulating blood filled every crevice of my body and there was an easy, rhythmic pulsing inside my hand without the ring.

Two women from catalog sales arrived at the doorway.

"Are you all right, miss?" asked a petite girl who had obviously moved here from somewhere else.

I smiled broadly, holding the ring as tightly as I could in my right hand. "I am quite fine, thank you."

"Should we call a doctor?" asked a tall red-haired preppy woman.

"No, I'm on my way to one right now." I left the building with the confident look of a woman whose credit line had been extended.

I ran down the avenue holding the ring in my cramping fist. The diamond was cloudy and emotionally tarnished when I placed it into the black velvet safety deposit box. This ring survived something that another might not, and so would I.

*   *   *

The doctor was horrified by the infection that oozed out of the wound when he cleaned it. I was delighted to watch my hand regurgitate the last bits of Steve's presence in my life. The doctor washed, scrubbed, rewashed, disinfected, and cleansed the hand until the pus that poured from it was transparent and clean.

I admired the creative way in which he wrapped the bandage so it lay flat on the hand. He had cut the fingers off of flesh-colored surgical gloves to protect the bandage and allow me maximum movement during the wedding. The nurse provided me with several bandages and altered gloves for my honeymoon. While I waited in my car across the street from Twisters Donuts, looking for a woman who might be Brittany, I realized my doctor was a homosexual. During all the years of noticing his perfectly buffed nails and the smells of his sweet hand creams, it had never occurred to me that everyone in his office was a man. I used to brag about going to see him because he was exquisite and his male nurses were handsome and divine. Stripping in front of them was a fantasy that had often distracted me from doing my homework as a young girl. Life was now a metamorphosis of jigsaw puzzles. The picture changed every time I laid down another piece.

A beautiful blond woman with a set of expensive luggage settled herself in front of Twisters Donuts. She sipped on a coffee and held a small white bag with grease stains. As I pulled out of a loading zone to cross the street I hoped that she had bought me a glazed doughnut instead of cream filled.

Brittany staggered awkwardly to the corner with her bags when she saw me waving to her across the mounting tunnel traffic. As I crossed four lanes of cars to reach her I bumped the back end of a police car. The officer stalked both cars and paced by my window seven times before giving me the signal everything was fine. He peeled out into the center of the lane in order to make two yards of progress in the thick car fumes.

"Rough week, huh?" She smiled encouragingly.

"Very."

"Do you want me to drive?" she asked.

"No. I just need a minute."

"Glazed and some coffee?"

"With cream?" I asked.

"I hope light without sugar is fine."

"Perfect."

We barely made it to the other side of the tunnel when the traffic slowed considerably. I groaned and wondered out loud if we should have taken the train.

"Why didn't you take the train all the way down to Philadelphia?" I asked Brittany.

"Susan said you shouldn't be alone."

I nodded. "What were you doing in Boston? I thought you were from the *Lake* region of Chicago."

"You're implying that I'm snotty and rich with that comment."

"Sort of. But you can't be too snotty if Susan likes you." I smiled.

"I needed to put something else on the burner," she sighed.

"What do you mean?" I asked, looking at the long line of license plates standing still and circling the bend to the New Jersey sports complex.

"*The burner,* like cooking things on a stove, I needed to diversify my attention."

"You mean like a rebound?"

"No. The rebound is what you have after you break the spell. Putting something on the burner is sleeping with someone else and not pretending it will go any further. A rebound is where you daydream about the future to make yourself feel better about having reckless, good sex." She reached into the glove compartment and took out a map.

"Is Boston a good city for that?"

"Any city is good as long as you have an ex-lover there or someone you always wanted to sleep with but never did."

"Paris might be nicer," I said.

"I loathe Parisians," she said, knocking a hard pack of cigarettes across the inside of her wrist.

"I've never been, but I put in my application to run the marathon there next year."

She drummed the cigarettes on her wrist twenty-two times before slipping off the cellophane wrapper.

"Can I have one of those?" I asked.

"What about the marathon?"

"I want one of those right now, and the marathon is next year." I chuckled slightly to myself, feeling the swell of rebellion. Steve hated smokers. He would make a big fuss in restaurants and wave his arms around in the air trying to rid himself of the secondhand smoke. Of course, he would suck enviously on a cigar if it was offered to him.

"It will kill you," she said.

"What won't?" I asked.

We smoked our cigarettes and listened to other people's radios. Brittany smoked hers fast and lit up another one. I lingered with mine, not knowing quite what to do with it but enjoying the stillness of what I inhaled. The cigarettes burned faster than the car moved in traffic. I didn't want to interrupt the silence between Brittany and me again. We both seemed compelled to pretend we were fine: smoking cigarettes, drinking coffee, staring out the windows, and flipping the radio station every time a love song came on. We were both growing impatient in the traffic standstill. The heat was escalating inside the car as the asphalt burned in the high sun. Brittany was like many women I knew. She had a confidence that could be intimidating if you didn't know she often doubted herself. She was like me, wearing hardened calloused exteriors marred by soft, pliable, pained hearts. I didn't want to understand any more about Brittany than I already knew because being in her company was like being closer to myself. I watched her fidget in traffic and put her right foot up on the dashboard.

"Get off at the next exit," she demanded.

"We're hours from the parkway intersection."

"Exactly. Clearly we're not getting anywhere on the turnpike, and since we are hours away from where we need to be, let's take the small roads."

"Even if the road is jammed and we're completely stopped, don't forget you're talking about New Jersey, not some cute country interstate in Illinois."

"Corn. Tomatoes. Fields. Fruit. What do you think?"

"Toxic waste. No, we need to get there." I shook my head in disbelief.

"We need to get there by Saturday at eight o'clock in the morning to have our hair done," she said.

I looked into her eyes. She was pleading, but conceding was never my strong point.

"Can you see other roads on that map?" I asked politely.

"Does it matter? If we head south we'll get close enough."

She didn't understand all the effort it took for me to entertain her idea, and now I resented her tone. "All this spontaneity is a nice idea, but honestly I've had a hard week and I can barely pay attention to the highway."

"Then let me drive." She got out of the car and walked around to my window.

Her assertiveness was neither amusing nor entertaining. "Get back in the car," I ordered, and took my foot off the brake and let it roll forward.

"Move over and let me drive." She stood alongside of the car as we inched forward.

"This isn't funny."

"You're right. It's life. Now you're on Brittany time. Brittany hasn't had a pretty week either, and she would like to forget about the laundry and the dry cleaning and the bills, and who gets the car, and why she is always left to clean up a mess other people make!"

My hand whitened in a fist around the wheel. I could see myself getting out of the car and punching her in the stomach with a right uppercut. She deserved it, but I knew it wasn't the same as hitting a man. Once you shattered a woman's exterior wall her emotions often escalated into hysteria, which is the real danger when fighting with one. I knew better than to push either of us right now.

"Brittany, please go to your side of the car and help me put the convertible top down."

"I want to drive," she insisted like a child.

"No one—and I mean no one—drives, or has driven, my cherry-red antique Mustang except the old man who sold it to me. You navigate and I drive or you can walk slowly behind me in this bumper-to-bumper traffic until we get to Pennsylvania."

"Are we getting off?" She put her hands on her hips.

"Yes," I sighed.

As Brittany walked around the front of the car she shook her long mane of blond hair several times. I noted that her arrogance suited the Mustang's polished chrome and insignia horse. It was why I cherished the car. There was no need to explain myself when people saw me drive it. Brittany did not get back in the car but walked alongside it. She knocked on the hoods and trunks of other autos to move people along. As we began to cut through the endless lines of stopped cars and edge our way onto the shoulder of the road, the other vehicles cleared for us as if we truly were wild horses lost on the New Jersey Turnpike.

Allowing Brittany to navigate was a further exercise in patience. She was a spoiled child wavering on the edge of a tantrum. I gave in to most of her whims because I was closer to real hysteria than she was. If I allowed myself to lose what sanity remained in my body I would never make it through Susan's wedding. I reminded myself often of this when stopped at a convenience store, a liquor store, and a drugstore. Brittany put her hands together in a prayer and pleaded like a little girl when she saw a farm stand ahead.

"Please, please stop by the booth."

"Do you have to pee?"

"No."

"Then why stop?"

"I have a surprise for you."

"Oh, please, I'm very tired of this month's surprises."

"I want to thank you for getting off the highway."

"And you'll do that by making me stop every fifteen minutes until you push the limit of my sanity?"

"This is the last one."

"Fine, if you ever have to pee you should know right now I'm going to make you hang your ass off the side of the car."

I knew she wanted to make a smart comment about how I probably *would* stop because I love my car so much, but she knew better, and I appreciated that she didn't push the limit any further. I pulled off the road in front of the leather-faced man standing in a white shack with a bright yellow sign over his head that read JERSEY TOMATOES.

Brittany returned to the car and motioned for me to collect the bags she had acquired at every pit stop. She also carried a large brown bag for us and staggered through rows of corn. I followed diligently behind her, asking no questions. The sun was still hot, and I lightly sweated into my slacks. Muddy trails splattered small bits of earth onto my clothing. When we came to the end of the cornrows a field of sweet green grass spread itself before us. There was a faint smell of manure and onions, but there were no cows.

"Anywhere special you would like to sit?" asked Brittany.

"Everywhere," I said.

"So be it."

We walked just a few more yards and settled onto the soft side of a hill. Brittany had a small army knife but used her fingers to do most of the work. She gutted four tomatoes and stuffed them with mayonnaise. At a package store she had purchased a bottle of young sparkling Italian wine and a bottle of French Beaujolais.

"Pick your poison," she said.

I looked up at the sun and knew the red wine would make me sad and keep tears in my eyes. "I'm actually a tremendous fan of the prosecco. I think the grape is clean and crisp. It would be nice to feel that clean, even if it was temporary."

"I was hoping you'd pick that one." She smiled.

She pulled two tall plastic champagne flutes from the paper bag.

"Nice touch! Where did you get those?" I asked.

"Even though package stores are an inconvenience to the adventurous traveler, they are good for alcohol paraphernalia."

I lay back in the grass and felt the rough manicured field below me. There were places where I perceived water soaking my blouse, but the cool earth comforted my back and the sun dropped a hot blanket over my face and arms. I felt the honeyed wet taste of the sharp grape on my lips and opened my eyes.

"You look so peaceful," she said.

"I am."

"It's a shame we're both so sad. This could be a beautiful place to make love."

My eyes must have opened wider and displayed some mixture of horror and shock.

"Don't worry, I wouldn't force you into anything. I don't even know you, but I like you. You have qualities that I search for in myself. Would you be mad if I kissed you?"

"Will you be mad if I'm not a lesbian?" I asked defensively.

"That's fine."

"Is that fine?"

"Of course."

She put her hand on my knee and gave it a small pat and then filled both flutes with wine. As she moved, it was easy to imagine there had been many men who wanted to kiss her, too.

"To the adventure," she said, raising her glass.

"I can drink to that. Brittany," I stuttered. "I, I, I have a lot on my mind, and I'm not sure that I won't, or I don't want to kiss you," I said.

"I'm not sure, either," she said.

She made me laugh at my seriousness. "I want to kiss you, but I don't want to. Or not right now, or . . ." I stumbled on my thoughts.

"How many guys have you kissed and walked away from?"

"Is it a pretty good kiss?"

She smiled. "You know what I'm asking. How many?"

"A lot."

"This isn't any different. We're having a beautiful moment, in a beautiful field, and we could have a beautiful kiss."

I laughed again with her. "Brittany, I don't know what Susan said to you, but—"

"Susan said to make sure you didn't spend the entire drive beating yourself up for not marrying a jerk. She said that of all her close friends she couldn't believe that we didn't know each other because we are the most compatible. She also said that it would make sense if you were a lesbian, but that you would have probably known by now." She paused. "By the way, if you are a lesbian, she wants to know why you have never *kissed* her."

"I've never been with a woman. Except for the girl I used to practice with in the third grade." I shrugged.

"I had one of those! Marianne Blush. What a great name. We used to practice for hours."

"Do you think everyone has one of those?"

"A lot of us did."

"You mean you and your lesbian friends did?" I asked tentatively.

"*No!* My friends with mothers who drank martinis in the afternoons. We made out to pass the time until they went shopping."

"Oh."

"I'm flattered you would consider me for your first kiss. However, I would have put money on the fact that you'd had several women as lovers before."

"Why?"

"Your demeanor."

"You mean because I'm all feminine, lace, big hair, pretty girl stuff, with lots of perfume and makeup?"

"How about all the strength and power and the inability to let yourself be vulnerable?"

Moving quickly I leaned forward and kissed her on the cheek. "Thank you."

"Thank you. I wouldn't be here if you had been some prig who wouldn't get off the exit ramp. It's nice to wander through the fields with someone, remembering that life does not end at the dry cleaners."

"Is that where we all figure out our relationships are over?" I realized two of Steve's ties were still at the downtown cleaners.

"It sure wasn't in therapy!" she laughed.

Brittany finished her wine and pushed the stem of my glass above my chin so I was forced to swallow the rest of mine. As she poured us another flute she said: "I was standing at the cleaners when I had this overwhelming desire to leave her clothing there. When I drove home I noticed the last person to clean the house was me, the last person to change the oil in the car was me, the last person to give a part of herself was me. I sat down and wept until the entire house had grown dark. The moon had risen high over the house and filled it with blue light. I couldn't remember the last time I was loved, or wanted to make love, or remembered to look at the sky. I cried some more until my partner came home and asked why I hadn't started the grill for dinner."

"And I wanted to stay on the turnpike . . . ," I said softly.

Brittany breathed through her tears and laughed. "I want a relationship where you pull off the highway and eat tomatoes."

"And drink wine, kiss, or lie in the grass together," I sighed.

"To Prince, or *Princess* Charming," she said, raising her glass in the air again.

13

Take This Woman

When we arrived at the hotel there was a message that the other bridesmaids were waiting for us in the bar. They were easy to find.

"What does a man call safe sex?"

"A padded headboard!"

Each woman was wearing a bright floral printed sarong tied loosely about her body and shifting uncomfortably in orange vinyl seats. Native costumes on Anglo Saxons imply a type of mockery. It requires a certain amount of poise and style to make someone else's strong cultural style look natural. The same could be said of bridesmaids dresses. They are abnormal costumes for anyone who has not already endured the rite of passage down the aisle.

"What do you call a man with half a brain?"

"Gifted!"

"What is the difference between a man and a catfish?"

"What?"

"One is a bottom-feeding scum sucker, and the other is a fish."

Jeannine was the first person to notice us and slid off her bar stool with several umbrellas stuffed in a drink she carried with her.

I smiled at Brittany. "Obviously we've come to the right place."

"What did God say after he created man?"

"I can do better."

"How was the drive?" asked Jeannine with a hearty hug and kiss.

Brittany and I nodded at each other. "Good."

"Did you decide to go off-roading or four-wheeling?" she asked, looking down at our muddy trousers.

"Corn picking," said Brittany.

"Go change so we can move out of this Howard Johnson lounge and head downtown."

"In our sarongs?" I asked.

"Go with it. Get an umbrella drink and get ready to forget." Jeannine gave me another long hug and then pushed me toward the door. When she was that overtly affectionate it was apparent to me something was on her mind.

"Why do men marry virgins?"

Brittany yelled back into the dark barroom: *"Because they can't stand criticism."*

In the elevator I stood close to Brittany and closed my eyes. I was tired from the drive. I had promised myself I wouldn't drink too much. I had promised myself that I'd make it through this weekend, and then I could lie on the beach for days in St. John and suck overpriced cocktails through a straw. I looked across the elevator at the polished silver doors. My reflection was stretched and distorted.

Twenty-nine felt ridiculously old. I told myself that women had babies at forty. I told myself that women were different *now.*

I never owned a Betty Crocker cookbook or Barbie dolls, and no one had come to repossess my vagina. As the elevator lurched upward, I felt weak and I swayed.

"Hey, hey, are you OK?" asked Brittany as the doors opened.

"I need to lie down," I said hopelessly.

"We'll lie down." She slipped her hands under my armpits and tried to lift me. "You can take a break from everything really soon. We just need to get to the room. Walk with me."

We traveled up and down the floor looking for our room. On our way I slid against the wall, gripping the solid mass of plasterboard and textured wallpaper, hoping that its stability could infiltrate my body. Once inside, I collapsed on the bed, staring at myself in the cheap hotel mirror. This wasn't me. This was someone else. I always rose to the occasion. I always pushed my emotions aside and handled a solid day's work. My closest friend was about to celebrate the most gracious union in the world, and I couldn't get off my knees.

"Is this physical or emotional?" asked Brittany, searching her bag for her sarong. "Should I call a doctor?"

"I just feel overwhelmed. I've never been this exhausted in my entire life. I could lie here all night and all day and order room service until I grew old and fat and never have to worry about finding a mate."

"Take your clothes off," ordered Brittany.

"What?"

"I'll take them off if you don't."

"I can't wear that scarf thing all night."

"You'll wear it, I'll wear it, we'll all look like pale island girls. We'll drink enough so that no one notices we feel like fools. Get undressed."

"Why can't we just get there late?"

"You, my dear, are going to collapse all weekend whether you realize it or not. You need to just keep moving. I see the signs. You think you should notify the *New York Times* because falling apart is such a big event. The headline should read STRONG WOMAN NOTICES HER PAIN: CRUMBLES UNDER ITS WEIGHT."

"The *New York Times* was already notified." I began to slowly undress, too slowly. Brittany had already stripped down, pinned up her hair, and rearranged her pocketbook essentials into a smaller "bitch" knapsack. She looked at me with frustration and started to take off my shoes. Quickly she had undone my slacks, slipped off my panties, unhitched my bra, and shoved my feet into a pair of gold sandals. When Jeannine walked in I was naked, standing with my arms spread wide like Jesus on the cross with each end of the sarong held in my palms. Brittany stood in front of my naked body barking orders and pushing my breasts flat with her forearm so I could pull the material tight enough across my chest for support. Jeannine gasped at first and then broke into hysterical giggles, spilling her umbrella drink down the front of her wrap. Jeannine rarely drank. This was not a good sign.

By the time Susan arrived at the restaurant, her entire bridesmaid party had decomposed into a mess of emotions and alcohol. I was not alone in my misery, which raised my spirits considerably. Brittany demanded her plight for happiness was the most harrowing because even after finding a mate, she still had to seduce someone to have a baby. There would also be the agony of which female partner would get to carry the baby, and whether or not they should let the father be involved in the rearing. Screaming at the top of our lungs, we invited any female who had a man-hating joke to join us.

"What do you call an intelligent man in America?"

"A tourist!"

Peals of laughter ripped through the restaurant.

"What do you have when you have two balls in your hand?"

"A man's undivided attention!"

I believe we were asked to leave soon after that and ignored the request.

"How many men does it take to put a roll of toilet paper on the hanger?"

"No one knows because it's never been done."

In the bathroom I washed my face and continued to search for the joy I wanted to feel for Susan. The alcohol-induced dazzle barely soothed the gnawing tears that hovered at the edge of my eyes. Susan was next to me in the mirror when I looked up from the sink basin.

"You're not yourself," she said.

"I've had too much to drink."

"You hold your liquor better than anyone I know."

"I haven't had *enough* to drink?" I pleaded.

"How are you?"

"Please, please, please don't ask. Please? I'm falling apart. I can barely stand up, I'm so exhausted by being a bridesmaid and an ex-fiancée. I want to be happy for you, but *I'm* so lost."

"Thank God. I thought you'd pull the whole 'I'm so strong' trip. At least you're being human." She reached out for my hand and grabbed the injured one.

"Ouch!"

"Hey, that is a great wrap job. I didn't even notice you had a bandage on. No one will be able to tell in the photographs."

"My French manicure will be a bit tricky." I smiled.

She waited in silence, knowing there was more.

"I need to talk to you, but I don't want to burden you now." I felt the quiver in my voice and I knew that tears would follow if I didn't stop articulating my distress.

"You're my best friend—you are never my burden," she said.

I threw my arms around her and held her so tight I wanted to climb inside her for refuge.

"What is it, Cece? Tell me."

"Do you believe in the fairy tale?"

"I'm about to get married, aren't I?"

"So you believe there is a perfect match for every person?"

"It depends on how you look at it," she sighed, and began to laugh. "As long as you don't think the perfect match means you'll find a perfect person."

"I believe that. It just seems like I can't separate the good buys from the bad bargains."

"Cece, you know you can't force it."

"Why does everyone else seem to be married now?"

"Because the panic is spreading." We both laughed. "Don't give in. You of all people just pushed away a "perfect" guy for someone else. He just wasn't perfect for you."

"My mom thinks I'm searching for something that doesn't exist. When Steve and I broke off our engagement it touched a nerve in her. She seemed to suddenly want to be there for me and at the same time convince me there were no perfect matches."

"First of all, you have had plenty of relationships. You're the most dedicated woman I know. You give everything. You just give it too fast. Don't start wandering around mumbling you need a therapist, you're unable to commit, or you can't have relationships."

I nodded. "I just don't want to compromise."

"Don't."

"But what . . ." I paused and took a breath to resist crying. "But what if I wind up alone?"

"Cece, you're better at being alone than anyone I ever knew."

"But I'm tired of it." The tears rolled gently from my eyes. "I'm tired of running alone, I'm tired of traveling alone, I'm tired of paying for lesson packages with instructors when I'm on holiday because I have no one else to talk to."

The more I talked, the more relieved I became. As I held Susan a growing sympathy for my parents rose inside me. The world they had come from was hypocritical and strict. I thought about the way my mother shrugged at the nuns when they complained of my behavior, and the resentful curl of my father's lip when he placed money in the collection basket. They had waited anxiously while I staggered from one relationship to the next in order to allow me to discover what was true for myself. My parents had ignored my late nights, held back their opinion, and removed themselves from my life. The neglect I had always assumed was selfishness on their part now appeared to be their only method of kindness. How often I had despised them and compared them to other parents, especially Susan's, accusing them of neglect and carrying resentment for their ineptitude. They wanted desperately to make sure that I needed no one else to survive and would never have to compromise. What they didn't understand was how hard it was now for me to invite someone else in.

"I'm going to be fine," I said, pulling away from Susan's embrace and forcing myself to stop crying.

"Sure you are, Cece. You're always fine. I just want you to be happy."

"Find me a six-foot-two, slender, freckle-faced Catholic rebel who likes to run, drink, make love, and won't tell me what to do."

We embraced in one last long rocking hug before several agitated women banged on the door screaming they had to urinate.

No one should have driven from Philadelphia to the suburbs. We were drunk and careless. We inhaled cigarettes like high school teenagers and blew smoke and hot ashes out the window. We turned the radio up and pulled over on the shoulder of the highway when we felt like tribal dancing barefoot in our printed sarongs with a collection of small frail umbrellas decorating our hair.

By the time we reached the hotel, we had separated the cars into two groups. The locals returned to the confines of their parents' houses and memories of coming home late, and visitors went to hotels with the sheets turned down. Jeannine was in the wrong car. When we spilled into the lobby of the Howard Johnson she clung to my side. We shuffled alongside one another in bare feet, down the hall toward the closed bar. Like a defeated team of athletes banished to the locker room, we turned and sulked back to the elevators. Jeannine was obviously making no effort to go home, and Brittany and I were ready to keep drinking.

"I'll stay with you, but I'm not sleeping naked," she stated with authority.

"Neither are we," said Brittany, more sober than I.

"Maybe I *should* sleep naked." She absently let her eyes fall on her engagement ring.

Brittany and I looked at each other and shook our heads.

"I don't think we have enough alcohol in the mini-bar," said Brittany.

"Alcohol, yes; coffee for tomorrow, no. What time is your manicure?" I asked distractedly.

"What time is your manicure? Will you wear the same dress as your sister? Are you having a Quaker wedding or a Catholic service? When is your bridal shower? Where have you registered?" asked Jeannine.

"When do we have to pick the flowers for the meetinghouse?" I asked.

"When do you know it's the real thing?" asked Jeannine, demanding attention.

"When are we going to bed?" asked Brittany.

"Bed?" I asked.

"Don't look so nervous. I meant sleep."

"Everyone was engaged. Everyone was making plans. I didn't even hesitate when he asked," said Jeannine, pounding lightly on the door of our hotel room.

"It always feels like that." I put my hand on her bare shoulder.

"Even when you're a lesbian," said Brittany, with her hand on the knob.

We entered the room and began a survey of the mini-bar. We removed our sarongs and slipped into oversize T-shirts and sweatpants. The titillation of being glamorous had worn off. Going home with other women meant the pressure to look good was over. The sexuality that had eased over the tops of our sarongs and crawled from the slits up the center of our wraps retreated into the safety of sleeping among one another. There were no facades to uphold or seductive positions to recline in around the hotel room. I didn't have to wash my face and apply traces of makeup so that when I awoke I didn't look like a tired whore. There was an allure and intensity to casual sex, but it became as old, and as exhausting, as pretending to swallow. Tonight, our hair went up in elastic bands, tightly pulled back away from our faces. We sat scrunched or hunched on a chair. We were sloppy and dropped things like peanuts, chips, ice cubes, bottle tops, and insults. We were annoyingly frank and often cruel, until Jeannine started to cry. It was obvious that fear was testing her ability to be rational as it often does for each of us.

We fell asleep entwined in a pretzel of limbs and were awoken shortly after our last words were spoken by an obnoxious harrowing of bells.

"Is Jeannine with you?" demanded Susan on the telephone.

"Uh, yes," I said.

"Well, at least she didn't sleep in another guy's hotel room. Having a *ménage à trois* with my two best friends is a much better excuse." Susan was exasperated.

"I think she liked it," yelled Brittany.

"What?"

"Aren't you ready for some hangover humor?" I asked quietly.

"You three ladies need to get your asses out of bed and be here to help me with this list of things I have to do."

"What happened to meditation?"

"Right, if I tried to sit down my body might explode."

"What about your other bridesmaids?"

"Useless. They won't answer the phone."

"Can you call back in ten minutes?"

"Why?"

"So I can *not* answer the phone."

"Get up. Bring doughnuts and bagels. People here are starving, and they are all stinky, cigar smelling, hungover men."

"Why don't you come over here and hang out by the pool?" I asked.

"Right, I'll just hang out while the rest of the world destroys my wedding. Please come save me from being a bride!"

"OK, we're coming in a little while."

"Now!"

14

Till Death
Do Us Part

My fingers were still bleeding even after the polish had dried. The esthetician had tried to cut away at the severity of my cuticles and calluses in order to apply a French manicure. I had been one of the first to volunteer at the salon because it would take energy and patience to deal with my hands. The years of carrying crates and hauling ropes were still visible in the dry cracked creases of my palms. At times I imagined the intense odor of fish was embedded in my skin like the smell of garlic and onions emanating from a cast-iron pot. No matter how much cream I applied to my hands or how many times I soaked them in hot wax hoping to soften their touch, they still shredded pantyhose and caught on fine fabrics. The woman who executed my manicure was exceedingly patient and humored by her challenge. She worked diligently around my bandages and although my nails were short (she had to fake the style of the manicure by painting on the outside of the nail) they looked attractive when she finished.

I paged through glamour magazines and read old horoscopes

until it began to rain. Clouds that loom and then open over Pennsylvania become storms that are filled with the moist intensity of the southern states and the modern panic of the north. Susan's eyes filled with tears.

"We haven't picked the flowers," she gasped.

"Rain on the rehearsal is a good omen!" cried one of the girls in the salon.

Susan's mother, sister, and surrounding neighbors had planted wildflowers in a plot that they had rented from a farmer last spring. Susan enjoyed field flowers and wanted natural arrangements on the tables. She had soaked only half a hand, and no fingers had been painted. Brittany was nursing her hangover and flirting with the cute petite redhead who stroked her hand during the manicure. Jeannine had a list of her own, the other bridesmaids were still in bed or hiding in the toilet, and my nails were dry.

"If Jeannine can drop me off at the farmer's plot, I can start clipping. She can do her errands and come back and get me," I volunteered.

"The flowers have to get to the country club today too for the arranger to put them together for the reception," worried Jeannine.

"I have nothing to do all afternoon except come up with a good toast for the wedding. I can cut the plot and wait for someone to bring me over to the club."

Susan smiled. "Call one of the groomsmen to come help her. Make sure he's single."

"I'm willing to risk my French manicure, the nicely wrapped bandages on my hand, and catch a cold; don't ruin it with a man."

"Don't worry, they're not all Deadheads. I think there might even be a Catholic guy."

"Very funny."

*   *   *

By the time Jeannine left me at the edge of their plot, the rain was an obstacle. It was heavy and pushing down on the veins of the flowers. The plot was large and hard to navigate. The neat rows of flowers had disappeared and begun to grow into a complicated labyrinth. I searched desperately for the bottom of each stem. It was necessary to save as many as possible to have enough for the reception and tomorrow's ceremony at the Quaker meeting-house. Struggling to delicately cut each flower and lay it in a protected area, I cursed the other bridesmaids.

I began cursing out loud in the rain. I cursed Brittany and the rest for being vain, for having lists, for not helping. I cursed Steve for the time I lost to him and I cursed myself for the men I had wasted myself on. There was a hymnal aspect to my shrieking that turned into a song I hadn't sung since my childhood at church. I made up my own words and stumbled forward with the tune.

Moving through the field, sinking deeper and deeper into my muddy tracks, I felt the weight of my ancestry. The tired earth was worn beneath my feet and my hands were not accustomed to handling objects that were so easily crushed. When I cut them properly, half the time I then managed to crush them on the way to their safe resting spot under a tree. My fingers longed for thick stems or roots. I would have felt more comfortable pulling rocks from the soil, or potatoes.

A strong voice called to me through the web of flowers and streaming rain. I was glad that whoever was coming to help me would not be able to decipher the difference between my tears and the thunderstorm.

"Should I put the ones you've cut into the truck? Or should I come help you first?"

"How many are you?"

"What?"

"How many of the groomsmen are here?" I asked impatiently.

"Just me."

"Oh, Christ! What the hell are they all doing, drinking beer?"

"I'm the only one they could spare, the rest are all being fitted at the tuxedo rental," he laughed.

I sighed. "I'm sorry."

"Where are you?"

"I'm somewhere between a homemade wedding and a mess."

"I'll come and help right after I load the truck with the flowers under the tree."

The tone of his voice made me question how I looked. Assessing myself as soaking wet, unraveling at the hand, dirt under the thin lip of my nails, a perfectly destroyed manicure, and the occasional bloodstain on my shorts from places where I had cut myself with the shears was not my ideal way to start a seduction. My own vanity amazed and horrified me. I wondered how much more abuse I wanted to incur before my honeymoon or if another one-night stand would prop my ego up for long enough to get through the weekend. A tiredness came over me and the ground beneath my feet started to spin. Going down onto my knees, I searched for my self-respect in the mud.

"Hey, I found you," he said.

"Oh, goody."

"Are you hurt?"

"I suppose. Exhausted is more like it. Tired of being a bridesmaid. There's no real glory to the job."

"What? You don't do it to wear those great dresses?" he asked with so much sarcastic humor, it made me want to stand up.

"I'm tired of being in the wedding, but never being the star. Does that make me sound formidable and selfish?"

He bent down to look at me. "No, it makes you sound real."

I put my muddy hand on his elbow and met his gaze. There was nothing that could have prepared me for who I saw. From the way he lurched backward, falling onto a handful of thorny rose bushes, I suppose there was nothing that could have prepared him, either. When we regained composure, we stared at each other in complete disbelief.

"*Catherine?*" he asked cautiously.

"*Johnny?*" My breath was shallow and panicked. I couldn't think, breathe, or move. Our faces were so close I could almost smell our past. Before I could stop my hand I slapped him *hard.*

"Did I deserve that?" he asked quietly without moving away from me.

"How much do you remember?" I asked.

"Everything," he said with conviction.

"Do you remember leaving me behind?"

He nodded.

"Do you remember how much my parents loved you, adored you, thought the sun and moon revolved around you?"

He nodded.

"How come you left us?" I asked.

"I couldn't stand up to it when they talked about you."

"Who?"

"Donavon, Mickey, Rich, you know."

"What did they say?"

"Come on, you know."

"I don't. I really don't know," I said with tears in my eyes.

"They were always talking about what weirdos your parents were."

I nodded.

"When you moved out of the neighborhood, everyone thought you were going to be a snob, too."

"Right? What a shame it is to want more in this life than a good beating with a belt and a beer tab at O'Neil's bar," I said sarcastically.

"We thought about union contracts not going to college—"

I laid my fingers on his lips. "Stop."

"What are you doing here?" he asked.

"I'm one of Susan's best friends. What are you doing here?" I asked.

"I'm one of Orin's best friends."

"This is not possible," I said. "How do you know him?"

"When I was figuring out what to do with my life, I hung out and followed the Dead. Do you know who they are?"

"I'm the one who went to college."

"Right." He nodded. "I loved the scene because it was so unlike everything I had experienced, but I was still in a rage, just a brawling Irish kid. I'd be drunk and start fights on the lawn all the time. One night, before a biker killed me, Orin reached into the center of the fight and plucked me out like the hand of God. The next thing I knew he set me up with a construction job and we lived by the beach for a year until I went back to school on the East Coast."

"Why didn't Susan tell me about you?"

"I'm married, remember? I was married then. I had run away from her and everything else."

I slowly shook my head in agreement. "Still married?"

"Divorce proceedings. And how are *your* wedding plans?"

I held up the bandaged hand that had unraveled and now exposed a deep purple wound. "I had a hard time getting the ring off," I said, shrugging my shoulders.

He took the hand and held it gently in his. "How do you know Susan?" he asked.

"We were in an educational program together at the United Nations when we were sixteen. We've been friends ever since."

"You never called me." He looked at the ground. "I actually thought you might since you had my business card. I jumped every time the phone rang in the office and checked my messages incessantly."

"I would have. I hid the card from myself until I figured things out with my ex-fiancé. It took me a few shots of Drambuie and a bottle of wine just to settle down after I had seen you."

"Are you sure you would have called?"

"Double sure." I hadn't said that in such a long time.

"I suppose we better pick the rest of these and drive over to the reception hall."

"I had almost forgotten," which was hard to believe since it was pouring rain and I was freezing.

"You've done a great job—we're really close to finished. Why don't you go warm up in the truck and I'll clip the rest?"

"No, let's do it together, OK?" I asked.

"Good."

I was walking the fine line between fate and reality as I staggered through the last few rows of flowers. These were the things that made me believe in God. These were the times I forgot why love caused pain and believed once again it caused only happiness. Something was happening that had no words or explanations. I was going to the trusting place again for no reason. He was for me. Perhaps for just today, for a moment, or years, but he was here to teach me something I needed to know.

"I think we're done," he said, dragging his sneaker along the remains of petals and flowers that could not be saved under the weight of the rain.

"Are *we?*" I asked.

"Here. We're done here."

As we bumped along in the truck he had borrowed from Susan's father, neither of us spoke much. We asked each other polite questions about turning up the heat or the window defrost. I was so cold my hand actually shrank to a normal size, and I imagined it healed.

We were thinking about everything that we had known about each other and everything we could piece together now. Waves of doubt swept over me followed by joyful optimism. After we unloaded the flowers at the reception hall, we returned to the truck and sat inside while watching the rain soak the greens of an adjacent golf course.

"I'm in awe," he said. "The words of Father Connelly are so clear in my head."

"What did he say?" I asked.

"I wanted forgiveness for my divorce, but you know they won't do that."

"Unless you're really rich."

"Or a Kennedy."

"True," I snickered.

"He wouldn't forgive me officially, but he did as a person. He said that we spend our entire lives meeting soul mates; we run into them, we date them; they are our friends; sometimes if we are lucky, they are our spouses. When we feel complete peace in a stranger's company it's a sign it's the right person, but the question is whether it's the right time."

"Are we strangers?" I heard a cautious tremor in my voice.

"On the subway everyone else was annoyed, irate, and unhappy. Sitting next to you, I felt a complete peace within myself and everyone else around us. All that time I didn't know who you were until the doors closed."

We leaned forward to kiss as if we had rehearsed this moment a thousand times before.

In the instant before our eyes closed and our lips pressed together he stopped. "I saw you once," he said.

"When?"

"A few years after you left. My dad had some business in the city, and I was down by the pier. I was trying to look cool, you know, smoking a cigarette. You walked by me carrying an anchor."

"It was probably lighter than it looked."

"You were sweating and your hair was pulled back. For a moment because of all the muscles in your arms, and some old sleeveless T-shirt you were wearing, I thought you were a guy. I'll never forget it. To myself I said, 'That is the most beautiful man I've ever seen.' You loaded things onto a scale and joked around with some Italian guy who grabbed at your crotch. My dad must have seen me watching because he came up and asked if I recognized you. He told me it was 'Crazy Catherine.' He said that your father had a fancy business and you'd probably go to college but for now you were a lowly dockhand like the rest of the kids."

Retreating to the corner of my seat, I pushed my head against the windowpane.

Johnny continued: "It was right around then that I started to realize that I was missing something in life. I tried so hard to get out. I even envied you for being free."

"I wish you told me why you ignored us back then."

"I would have never been able to pinpoint that I needed my

friends' approval, and I thought the farther I stayed away, the less I would hurt you."

"That seems like a funny thing to say, doesn't it?" I asked.

"Yes. I guess so."

I wanted to be closer to Johnny, but I was afraid of moving at all.

"You think you're the only one who remembers what we did?" His voice pitched into a deep discontent. "I could never get a woman to tell me exactly what she wanted."

"I don't understand."

"Women who want relationships spend so much time trying to please a man that they don't ask for what they need until it's too late. It seems only if a woman knows she'll be laying a guy once, she is precise about what she wants. I only found sluts who liked to talk dirty and tell you exactly *how* to fuck them and *where*—"

"So what was I?"

"You were my equal."

"Please don't use that word."

"I've waited for some woman who can tell me what she liked and disliked without feeling vulnerable. I became accustomed to one-night stands. Marriage to a good Catholic girl and the need to only wander on occasion seemed like a solution."

"That is not all my fault," I defended.

"Really? You had the book."

"You had the dream about screwing the widow Santiago."

He smiled. "You remember everything, don't you?"

"I remember that after you left my house it was so lonely I swore never to let anyone else in."

"Part of me wants to say, '*Hey, we were fourteen years old— what were we thinking?*' But I know it wasn't like that."

"If you were tortured all this time by your memories, and you knew where I was, why didn't you come looking for me?" I asked.

"Who still believes in fairy tales, Catherine?"

There was a long silence between us.

"If you're as tired of being alone as I am, you'll take your hand off the door latch and stop planning your escape." He held his hand out for me to take it.

I hadn't even noticed my fingers had moved to the handle and gripped it tightly.

"Do you want to miss this opportunity and then find out it was our last chance?"

Although I had been waiting my whole life to have him back, I opened the truck door and lingered until my arms were soaked again and a wave of thunder rolled through my bones. My mind told me to walk the thirty-seven miles back to my hotel, but for once my heart would not listen. I shut the door on the rain outside and moved toward him on the damp seat.

Acknowledgments

An author's first novel is the reflection of people, places, and ideas that have influenced the individual's life. I extend my deepest gratitude to:

Mentors: The wisdom of my agent Simon Green, and the guidance of Dan Green, both of whom I would never know, respect, and cherish without an introduction arranged by Frederick Reiken. I am awed by the strength of character and critical clarity of my editor, Laurie Chittenden. There would have been no incentive to succeed in the literary world without the knowledge passed along to me by Craig Nova, Edward Hoagland, Michael O'Donoghue, Bob Guccione Jr., Phebe Chao, Elizabeth Coleman, Phillip Lopate, James Lasdun, Richard Locke, Peter Cameron, Le Anne Schrieber, Rebecca Goldstein, Helen Schulman, Ethan Canin, Annie Blythe, Alice Wingert, David Bourns, John Ment, and the deep breaths of David Swenson.

Wonder Women: To Kathryn and Jessica Hoffman, the sisters who put me back together when I fell apart. I am also honored by the love I receive from Valerie Marcus, Samantha Gold, Erica Herman, Michelle Bogin, Maria Rosenblum, Courtney Baker, Laura Gevanter, Hannah McCouch, Amanda Gersh, Jennifer Lucas, Rachelle O'Connell, Bella Gerber, Rosie Wagner, Andrea Scheithauer, Pippe Bruess, Karin Granner, Evelyn Petros, and Beverly "Woodstock" Davis.

Super Men: I am grateful every day for the gem I married, Alexander Hruby, and the friendships of Tom Paine, Ken Foster, Michael Andrew Pascal, Ray Haboush, Alexander Kwit, Brian Katz, Matthew Ellis, Florian Sachiisthal, Dustin Schell, Albert Simmons, Ernesto Rodriguez, and Chris Newman.

Family: I am forever in debt to my mother, Eve Van Syckle, and her special policy of nonjudgment. I would not have reached my goals without the embraces of Elizabeth Caro, Peter Keller, Jeff Le Fevre, Joan Snitzer, Chouteau Merrill, Suzanne Rubin, Valentine Bureau, Cheryl Hardwick, Holly and Hugh McKracken, Susan and Bob Hoffman, Christa and Heinz Hruby, Mary and Marc Walsh, the Abrams, the Bucks, the Le Fevres, the Fassinis, the Orzacks, the Winters, my Berkshire School students, and the unquestionable strength of the Van Syckle tribe: Peter, Lorraine, Kim, and Richard.

Publications: An editor or publication usually delivers hope when doubt takes over the spirit of a writer. I will never forget the voices of Lois Rosenthal, *Story Magazine;* Melanie Rigney, *Writer's Digest;* Lauren Hicks Shelley, *Garden Design;* Jennifer Niesslein and Stephanie Wilkinson, *Brain, Child;* Rebecca T. Godwin and Art Flanagan, *Quadrille.*

Image Specialist: The joys of being a novelist are the numerous days you can avoid getting dressed, remaining in your study with unkempt hair. I am indebted to Charlie Green and her talents as a makeup artist and to Marion Ettlinger for her perspective and ability to bring forth the color of my character in black and white.

Institutions: Success is measured in many ways; I measure mine by the time I spent at the Ethical Culture Schools, George School, Bennington College, Columbia University, Thurber House, and Mike's American Bar & Grill.

ANDES HRUBY was born in Venezuela, grew up in New York, attended prep school in Pennsylvania, went to college in Vermont, and completed her graduate studies in New York City. She now divides her time between Austria, Connecticut, and Costa Rica.